THE MANY
DEATHS
OF
CYAN WRAITHWATE

THE MANY
DEATHS
OF
CYAN WRAITHWATE

R. PEREZ DE PEREDA

The Many Deaths of Cyan Wraithwate
Published by Darkwater Syndicate, Inc.
8004 NW 154 Street #623
Miami Lakes, FL 33016

www.DarkwaterSyndicate.com

Library of Congress Control Number: 2014933073
ISBN-10: 0-9910745-2-1
ISBN-13: 978-0-9910745-2-5

DEDICATION

For my children, Roque and Petra.

PREFACE

The story you are about to read was written in 1967, in Spanish, on a hand-me-down Smith-Corona typewriter. Before it could be published, life intervened—as life has a habit of doing—and the author set aside his dreams of becoming a published author. The story sat forgotten at the bottom of a desk drawer for over forty years, only now to see the light of day.

The author and the editing team at Darkwater Syndicate have endeavored to provide you with an English translation that most closely follows the spirit and flow of the original text, given that it was originally written in Spanish, and the writing conventions of the day have changed in the intervening decades.

We are pleased with the result, and hope you will be too.

—R. Perez de Pereda

I

Cyan Wraithwate's campaign in the Elashi Southlands had come to a standstill. He was loath to admit it, even to himself, but he was terrified.

The battle fought a week from yesterday brought him closer to death than ever before. A chance arrow struck him dead-center in the chest, punching clear through his breastplate, knocking him off his horse. He awoke hours later in his tent, his wounded chest swollen and warm, in frightening contrast to how clammy he felt.

He sat cross-legged in his tent, elbows propped on his thighs, face in his hands.

He hadn't left his tent in days.

A rustle at the tent's entrance drew his attention.

"This had better be important," Cyan spoke into his hands.

"Good evening, Captain Cyan," said his visitor.

He did not recognize this man's voice. Cyan raised his head.

Standing by the tent flap was a lanky wisp of a man enveloped in yellow robes. Every inch of him was draped in yellow fabric except for his clean-shaven head.

1

Cyan frowned. No doubt this man was a wizard. Cyan had never met a wizard he liked, much less would trust with anything more important than latrine duty.

"Why are you here?" Cyan asked.

The man paced inside with an imperious air. "General Godfrey sent me. He is disappointed over the news that his shining young protégé has lost impetus."

"If all he sent you out here to do is recite the obvious, then you can save your breath and leave."

The man drilled into Cyan with his steel blue eyes. "I am known as Wren. And I did not come solely to discuss the obvious."

Wren reached over his shoulder and slung off a small shoulder pack. He withdrew a forearm bracer polished to a high gleam. Two serpents were embossed into the metal. One coiled into a horizontal figure-eight pattern and the other did likewise, but vertically, bisecting the first.

Cyan's eyes flitted down at the armor and back up to meet Wren's. "Apparently, you got your facts wrong," he shouted, yanking his shirt open to reveal the bandages on his chest.

"You jump to conclusions," said Wren. "Wear this, and you need not don any more armor."

"You're a closeted academic."

"Is it that you are afraid?"

2

"You're wasting my time."

"See that I'm right," Wren spoke over him. "Try it on."

Cyan held his tongue, but shot Wren such a look of derision as would make a nun faint. Grudgingly, he obliged. The bracer fit as though it was made just for him; the leather straps did not even need adjusting to fasten the armor to his forearm.

"And now?" Cyan asked.

"Now we do a test," said Wren, an instant before snatching a dagger from beneath the folds of his robe. Cyan roared with surprise as Wren's knife flashed before him. A chill entered his body through his neck.

Cyan fell, cupping his wound with his hands. Blood surged between his fingers. Everything went gray, then black.

* * *

Cyan awoke with a start and kicked off the ground, springing to his feet and hollering all the while. Wren pointed his fingers and launched a smoldering ray of fire at Cyan that exploded at his chest. The burst knocked Cyan head over heels, landing him onto his back with the wind knocked out of him.

It hurt too much to move. Cyan's body let up wisps smoke.

"I am going to kill you for that," he wheezed.

"For what?" Wren asked, arrogant as ever.

"For…" Cyan trailed off.

"For killing you?" Wren suggested.

"Yes."

"But did I really kill you?"

"No," Cyan stammered. "No, I suppose not."

Damn Wren for being right, he spoke the truth. Cyan touched his injured neck and found that the flesh there was intact. Even the puncture wound in his chest was gone.

"Now you see the power of the bracer," said the mage. "Each time you are laid low, it will bring you back and grant you monstrous strength. But there is a catch."

"Isn't there always?"

"You must not take the bracer off," Wren said with emphasis.

Groaning, Cyan brought himself to sit up. "Is that all?"

Wren nodded.

"Good. Get out of my sight."

II

Daybreak saw Cyan astride his horse at the head of his army. His troops fell into position around the palisade wall of an Elashi hamlet. This would be a difficult siege. The week-long hiatus had given the defenders plenty of time to make preparations.

He called out to the people behind the walls, "Open your gates and surrender, and we shall be lenient with you. Refuse, and we will burn you out of your homes."

The Elashi men on the palisade catwalks held out both hands with their middle fingers up. Cyan was unfamiliar with Elashi culture but knew enough to recognize this for a rude gesture.

He gritted his teeth. "You brought this upon yourselves!"

Raising his battle-ax, Cyan gave the signal for the battering ram to advance. His army gave way to a crew of engineers pushing a wheeled ram. The engineers butted the device up against the palisade gates, then rocked the ram's head back on its fulcrum to send it careening into the fortifications. The ram stuck the gate with a deafening crack of splintered wood.

Coarse yells went up just as the ram smashed the gate. Cyan's horse reared as Elashi ambushers surged from out of hiding behind the palisade's blind spots. The ambushers fell upon the siege engineers' flanks like a wave at sea, utterly cutting the hapless men down.

Suddenly the sky darkened as though by a swift moving cloud. Cyan looked up, for a moment taking his eyes off the action, and saw that iron barbs rained down upon them.

He had led his men into a trap.

Cyan tugged on the reins and his mount threw him to the dirt. His shoulder gave a sharp pop on hitting the ground. Wincing, he dragged himself along one-handed, fleeing from the defenders' charge. His horse gave a panicked scream as the hail of falling arrows tore into its flesh. It reared again and toppled over onto Cyan, crushing him under its weight.

* * *

He awoke in a panic. Facedown and gasping for breath, he spun onto his backside and sat up.

The sun was half set. The battle was over. The bodies of an entire Elashi legion were fanned out in a circle around him, with him at the center.

Cyan stood. The palisade was leveled. Beyond it, waning daylight shone through black billows of smoke as the Elashi settlement burned.

"By Nordon," he whispered. Had he done this? He wasn't sure. He held up his forearm for a better look at his enchanted bracer, turned it one way then the other for any clues it might hold.

This was too much. Wren had gone too far. Cyan's orders were to subdue the Elashis, not to decimate them. It might be years before the Elashis would be in any shape to offer up regular tribute. This would get Cyan court-martialed for sure.

He tugged at the bracer's leather straps. As he undid the first band the bracer began to grow warm.

"What the...?" he muttered, then broke into a scream. The bracer glowed with searing heat like a blacksmith's forge. Smoke rose from his burning flesh. Cyan clasped the bracer with his other hand to yank it free but scalded himself and tore his hand away.

As abruptly as it began, the burning sensation stopped. The bracer had become a sooty black color. The leather straps that fastened it to his arm were gone. It had become a solid metal tube fused to his skin.

The world spun. Cyan clutched at his temples. His vision rippled as though running water fell before his eyes. When finally his senses settled down, he realized he was no longer in his tent. Cyan stood in a cavernous library. Books were stacked in shelves that ran floor to ceiling as far as he could see.

He was not alone.

"You tried to take the bracer off, didn't you?" said Wren in a matter-of-fact tone.

Cyan spun to face him. "You!" he bellowed. "You tricked me!"

"Did I?" Wren asked. "I gave fair warning against taking it off."

"You didn't say this would happen."

"I felt I didn't need to."

Cyan glowered at him.

"Was I not perfectly clear?" Wren went on.

"Then how did you expect me to take it off once I was through with it?" Cyan asked.

"It would have been simple, if you had come to me first."

Touché, Cyan thought. "What do you mean by would have been?"

Wren frowned at having to state the obvious. "I mean, it's now going to be a lot harder to take it off."

"So do it," said Cyan.

"I can't."

"What do you mean you can't?" he shot back.

"It's too late for me to do that now."

Cyan reached between his shoulder blades and drew his ax. "I don't have patience for your word games, wizard. So you'd better start making sense before I cut it out of you."

"You don't understand the powers at work here," Wren explained. "That one bracer has more power infused in it than any living creature can ever imagine. With it on you can be like a god, undying and eternal. But to safeguard against someone taking this power from its wearer, it binds itself to the flesh of the user when someone attempts to remove it."

Cyan eased his stance, lowered his ax slightly. "So I'm a god now, am I?"

"You are immortal," said Wren.

"For how long?"

"For as long as you are alive."

"That's forever, right?"

"So long as you wear the bracer."

"What if it comes off?"

"It won't."

"So then I'm a god?"

"Maybe."

"Answer my questions!"

"I thought I had," Wren drawled. He clasped his hands at his chest. "You will forgive me, as I am very busy. There is other work I must attend to. Should you need further assistance, merely call my name."

Wren extended a hand and a small white card popped into being between his fingers. Cyan took it and glanced it over. Printed on the card was the mage's name and occupation — Wren, Owl Mage.

"So now what …" Cyan began, and cut off. He was back on the outskirts of the Elashi village. Wren and his library were nowhere to be seen.

"Hmph. Wizards. Always here one minute and gone the next."

III

Cyan yawned. It was late and the moon was high. Such a thing for a god to require sleep, he thought. He trudged into the village and spent the night in the burnt-out shell of a house.

He slept a scant few hours before the sky burned rosy orange from the rising sun. His pupils stung in the morning light. Cyan rolled over and faced the wall. Today he had no reason to wake up early. His campaign was over and so was his career—not that a god needed such things.

It was not too long after that Cyan finally roused. His parched throat yearned for water. He felt like he hadn't had a drink in weeks.

He rubbed the sleep out of his eyes with the heels of his palms and stopped in mid-motion. The touch of cold iron against both sides of his face prickled his skin. Eyes still cupped, he blinked, then slowly drew his hands away from his face.

Both arms were covered in iron up to his elbows.

Cyan shook his head. He held up his left arm for a closer look at the bracer. On this arm was the one Wren had given him, he was sure of it—it was embossed with coiled snakes. The bracer on his other

11

arm wasn't there yesterday. He held it up, searched for buckles and found none.

"H-how?" he stammered. Cyan clasped his mouth with one hand, staggered backward and fell on his backside. Raspy little breaths wheezed through his fingers. He rapped on new bracer with his opposite fist. It sounded hollow.

"How can this be?" He held his arm out and turned it around. His right arm from his elbow to his fingertips was encased in iron.

He felt the need to scream. At that instant, Cyan cocked his head back, clenched his eyes shut yelled Wren's name.

When he opened his eyes he was in a dark, stuffy laboratory. Fumes rose from cauldrons and open beakers, making the atmosphere heavy. Wren sat at his desk, looking more amused than surprised. His workspace was cluttered with notes and papers stacked messily atop it and peeking out from its overfilled drawers.

"I take it that you are having some kind of trouble?" Wren asked.

"Oh not at all," Cyan said with a sarcastic grin, "unless you call my skin turning to lifeless metal trouble!" He held up both arms. "Look!"

"Such is the price of immortality. Did you think it would come without a cost?"

"This is not what I signed up for."

Wren spread his arms. "What is more timeless than iron? Iron does not die. And with proper care, iron never corrodes. Look at all the statues of war heroes—they're all made of iron for a reason. And now you can be just like them."

A fine sweat broke on Cyan's brow. He was not sure whether Wren had meant Cyan would end up like the war heroes or their statues.

"I don't want this," said Cyan. "I want my body back."

Wren steepled his fingers. "I'm sorry."

"What do…"

"I said I'm sorry," Wren spoke over him.

"That's not good enough!" Cyan shouted.

Wren's eyebrows dipped sharply at the inner corners. "It is not possible to reverse the effects of the bracer now," he said flatly.

"There has to be a way."

"There isn't. No mortal has the power to undo the magic that binds the bracer to you…"

Cyan grit his teeth. "Then who does?"

Wren's mouth pressed into a tight line.

"Damn it, you know something I don't, don't you?" Cyan yelled. He reached across the desk and grabbed Wren by the collar, dragged him across the desktop.

"Tell me what I need to know!" Cyan shouted into Wren's face.

"Cyan…"

"What?!" He shook the mage to rattle the answer out of him.

"There…" Wren stammered. "There exist four sage dragons."

"Quit with the fairy tales, wizard. Dragons don't exist."

"They do exist!" Wren clutched Cyan's wrists in his hands. Much as he struggled, he could not wrest free of Cyan's grip.

Cyan cocked back a fist.

"I'm telling the truth!" said Wren.

Cyan drilled his eyes into the wizard's quivering face. If Wren spoke any lies, he would have detected them by now. "Keep talking, wizard."

Wren's eyes flitted between Cyan's and his fist. "Four sage dragons guard the treasures of the elements—earth, wind, water, and fire. With their powers you can undo the binding force of the bracer, maybe even revert your metal body back to flesh."

"How do I find them?"

"Put me down first."

"How do I find them?" Cyan repeated, shaking the mage with each word.

"I will give you a charm…"

"Oh no," he cut him short. "Not that again. I'm through with magic."

"No, no, it's harmless, really! Trust me!" Wren pleaded.

"Unless I try to take it off, right? Then what'll happen? For all I know you could be giving me something that will phase me out of existence for good."

"No, this charm is completely safe, I promise. Now please, put me down so I can get it for you."

Cyan paused a beat, then shoved Wren back across the desk. Wren rolled off the workspace and onto the floor. The wizard got to his feet and dusted himself off.

"Right... well..." Wren trailed off.

Cyan gave a slow, deliberate nod. Even without words, the message was clear: "Get on with it."

Wren went to his cluttered chest of drawers and dug through them, spilling papers onto the floor. "I found it," he said, holding up a crude necklace. It was nothing more than a loop of jade suspended from a cord.

"Put this around your neck," Wren said, handing it to him. "It's a wind charm. It will take you wherever you want to go instantly."

Cyan opened his mouth to speak.

"And no, nothing will happen to you if you try to take it off," Wren preempted him.

It was with no slight trepidation that Cyan slung the necklace on. To his relief, the wizard had told the full truth this time. Nothing utterly detrimental had stricken him. Yet.

"What do I do once I've talked to the dragons?" Cyan asked.

"You need for them to lend you their treasures, each representative of the elements they stand for."

"I need one treasure from any one of them?"

"No." Wren hesitated. "All of them."

Cyan scowled.

"They will test you," Wren went on, "to see if you are worthy of their gifts. Once you have all four you must return here, and using their combined powers I might just be able to free you from the bracer."

Arms crossed, Cyan could not believe what he was hearing. Dragons did not exist — they never did. They were beasts slain by knights in fairy tales. He shook his head. Almost as unbelievable was that, for a moment, Cyan actually thought Wren was telling the truth.

He gave a sigh. "What do these treasures look like?"

"No one knows," said Wren. "No one has ever seen them.

Cyan nodded. "So now what?"

Wren froze in the middle of straightening the creases in his robe. "Tell the wind charm where you want to go."

It occurred to Cyan that he didn't know where any of the dragons were.

"You're overthinking this," Wren said. "Just tell it you want to go to the abode of the earth dragon."

"Why should I go there first?"

Wren threw up his arms in exasperation. "Stop making this difficult. Just go."

Cyan snatched up the charm and gripped it in his fist. "If this thing drops me into a fiery volcano, I'm going to claw my way out and come after you personally."

It was faint, but Cyan saw Wren's throat bob as the wizard swallowed hard.

The charm glowed bright green in Cyan's hand. Wren's papers rustled as a gust of wind kicked up, swirled into a vortex that began to whirl around Cyan. The world beyond the rush of air stretched into streaks of color.

"A final word of caution..." Wren shouted over the noise. "Try not to die too many times."

"Or else what?" Cyan yelled back.

"I'm not sure," said Wren.

That very second there was a bright flash of green and the next thing he knew he was falling to the ground face first.

IV

Cyan fell from a height of six feet and landed head down into a soft floor of wet leaves, getting a mouthful of them. He leapt to his feet and wiped his face clean.

Massive trees surrounded him, most so wide across that he could put both his arms around their trunks and not have them meet in the middle. Up above, the tops of the trees were lost beyond the mesh of lower branches that prevented the light from shining through except for tiny pinholes here and there. A mess of dead leaves littered the ground beneath his feet, forming a carpet of decaying vegetation that yielded to his weight. With each step he felt as though the ground would give way and he would sink to his waist into that moldy earth.

He was in the oldest, darkest part of a forest, where his mother told him never to play when he was younger. Fairy tales spoke of places like these, where evil witches and ravenous wolfmen made their home.

He shuddered.

"My ax!" he said, realizing his weapon was nowhere to be found. Just how did Wren expect him to do battle with so powerful creatures as these dragons without his trusted weapon? More than ever, Cyan knew wizards were closeted academics with no grounding on how things were supposed to get done.

Suddenly there came a whistling sound from the heavens. Something large and heavy barreled through the forest canopy, rending a hole through the treetops. His ax buried itself halfway into the forest floor. A shaft of sunlight shone upon it through the hole in the treetops as though it were the holy sword of the king. He pulled it free and brushed off the mud before slinging it across his back.

After a short walk he arrived at the doorstep to a structure seemingly cut from a solid block of white stone. He could see so signs of brick and mortar. If the structure was in fact carved from a single block, then the boulder was one of massive proportions. The roof of the building soared twenty feet into the air, culminating in a rounded peak. Its width and breadth were incalculable from where he stood. The building was a perfect dome. This had to be the earth dragon's shrine. It would make an equally fantastic mausoleum.

The double doors were unlocked. He pushed one open and looked for any signs of trouble inside before proceeding, his ax at the ready. A dense, musty forest smell pervaded the inner chamber.

Moss grew on the grout between the green floor tiles. Stained glass windows set in the dome's ceiling cast kaleidoscopic images onto the floor below.

Cyan glanced down at the images every now and then. One showed an ancient tree reaching skyward, its leaves all green and its massive, gnarled trunk a healthy brown. The next one depicted a wave at sea in bright blue. A third image was a blaze of orange and red. All in all there were six images portrayed, arranged in a circle.

Another pair of doors lay before him, no doubt leading to the earth dragon. He grabbed the brass ring mounted on one of the doors and pulled. The door would not budge. Frustrated, he hacked away at the wooden doors with his ax, leaving only superficial marks on their surfaces which magically sealed back up again.

"Come out, I know you're in there," he yelled.

"Entry lies through me," said a voice from behind him. He spun around and came eye-to-eye with a wolfman, much like ones his mother had warned him about years ago. Shaggy gray fur covered his body and peeked out from beneath the panels of his iron breastplate. He stood erect on two paws with his arms crossed, watching Cyan with deep set yellow eyes. A sword hung sheathed at his hip.

"I am Lupine, guardian of the shrine of earth," said the wolfman in an icily cordial tone. "State your reason for coming."

"I have come to see the dragon of the shrine."

"What business have you with my master?" The wolfman sniffed the air. "I sense anger in your heart, you have no doubt come to cause the master of the shrine harm."

"And I take it you will try to stop me?"

"That I will," said Lupine, snarling as he tore his blade from the scabbard.

"Lupine, stop!" boomed a voice that echoed throughout the shrine. "Let the stranger come. I shall deal with him myself."

Lupine bared his fangs. "As you wish," he muttered, putting away his sword. He did not take his eyes off of Cyan as we went for the door and pulled it open.

It struck Cyan as odd that he could not get the door to budge, yet it gave Lupine no trouble at all. Strange magic was at work here.

Lupine motioned for him to enter. The moment Cyan was inside the sanctuary, the doors closed behind him, barring his exit.

Cyan stood at the very heart of the earth shrine. The floor was no longer tiled, but instead consisted of finely packed brown clay. Far, far up above was the domed top of the building. Mounted in the center of the dome was a large stained glass ceiling mosaic that cast the image of the tree Cyan had seen earlier, but enormous in size. The image occupied most of the chamber's floor space.

The ground shook. A deep rumbling emanated from beneath the ground of the inner sanctum, as though the earth itself were growling with anger. Cyan crouched low to maintain balance during the quake, but was knocked onto his rear as a huge mound of soil rose up from the ground. When the trembling had ceased, his gaze came upon a mountain of raised earth. Soil trickled down the sides of the mound, first grain by grain then in long streams, until at last the outline of a very large four-limbed creature emerged from beneath the dirt. The creature shook off the remaining soil on its scales, and that was when Cyan realized he was face to face with the earth dragon.

He was huge. Cyan gawked as the green-scaled dragon brushed itself off then stretched each of his limbs one by one. The heart of the shrine, large as it was, seemed much smaller with the dragon present. The dragon measured no less than twenty feet long and eight feet in height, by Cyan's reckoning.

The dragon lay down on his belly and watched Cyan with his gargantuan blue eyes.

"I know why you have come here," the dragon said. "And it is not to pay me a friendly visit."

Cyan stood and reached back, fumbled for the handle of his ax.

"You want my treasure, don't you?" the dragon asked.

"Y-yes."

The dragon gave a deep sigh. "The medal of earth housed in this shrine helps maintain harmony and balance in nature. In the hands of a good man it can do much good, but in the hands of an evil man it can bring only pain. In you I sense a great anger. Though I cannot accurately divine your reasons for wanting my treasure, I know enough to tell that you are not worthy of it."

Cyan flushed. Bile rose in his throat. The nerve of this dragon to tell him he was not worthy! He clenched his jaw and tried his best at not betraying how furious he was.

"I am terribly sorry if you were inconvenienced by having to come all the way out here and return empty handed," the dragon continued. "Is there any other way that I may be of service to you?"

"Tell me your name dragon," he requested, not a hint of anger in his voice.

"My name?" the dragon parroted, slightly taken aback. "Very well. I am Malaya."

"Well, Malaya, today is the day you die!" Cyan gripped his ax in both hands and sent up a war cry.

The dragon was not impressed. "You plan to kill me?"

Cyan primed his ax for a sweep, aiming to sever the dragon's head at the base of his neck. He followed through with a half-circle swing that spun him fully around. The ax had failed find purchase — Malaya had vanished into a cloud of fine soil. Streaks of dust trailed Cyan's ax through the air.

"Show yourself!" Cyan yelled. "Let's finish this now!"

"This battle can only have one end," Malaya said, materializing out of the earth to Cyan's left. "And that is with your undoing."

"I think not!" he said, cutting off in a yell as he hefted his axe. The blade bit into Malaya's forearm just as the dragon turned himself into solid stone. The shrill peal of metal against stone echoed within the sanctuary. The impact sent painful tremors into Cyan's arms. He reeled, dropping his ax to the ground as he staggered backwards and fell over.

"You're too persistent for my liking," said Malaya, reverting to his normal self. "From earth were you made, and to it you shall return."

The ground beneath Cyan became very soft. To his horror he found he was sinking straight into the earth. He clawed at the dirt as it swallowed him but his fingers merely dug runnels in the soil. Soon he was up to his head, then that too went under until no trace of him was left.

There was no air. There was no light. Streams of dirt ran down his throat and nostrils. All around and inside him, the dirt was hardening, turning to stone, crushing his body. He would die in his own grave—a practicality he might have appreciated were it happening to someone else.

The packed earth tightened, squeezing the breath out of him, collapsing him into himself, tighter, tighter, until…

Pop.

* * *

New life coursed through Cyan's veins immediately. Along with life came massive strength. Cyan clawed through the earth with his bare hands.

He pulled himself out of the ground snarling like a wild animal. His muscles burned with inhuman energy, his vision was stained red. Red was the one color he most wanted to see anyway. Only one thing was on his mind now—he would kill.

Before the startled dragon could defend himself, Cyan had already snatched his ax off the ground and swung it one-handed. The blade cut through the air, taking with it the head of the dragon guardian, severed neatly at the base of the neck. Malaya's head bounced across the floor, spraying blood everywhere.

Malaya's body did not collapse.

"Now look at what you've done," said Malaya's head, lying sideways on the floor. "What am I supposed to do, place my head above a mantle as a trophy? Yes, that's it—perhaps when I have company I can sit down and talk about it as it rests up there above my fireplace."

"Why don't you die?" Cyan shot back.

Malaya picked his head up with one claw. "Oh that's being considerate. You've decapitated me and now I'll bleed as much as I care to. Like I was saying, how do you expect me to breathe fire now? If only you knew how cold winters get around here. Winters are harsh without a source of warmth."

"Shut up! Just shut up and die! Please!"

"I cannot die!" Malaya roared, thrusting his head at Cyan to drive the point home.

"Then maybe this will help!" he yelled, and hacked into the dragon's left shoulder with a mighty downswing. The murderously sharp ax hewed into green scaled flesh, taking Malaya's arm. It flopped on the ground like a severed lizard's tail.

"You are becoming quite a nuisance," said Malaya, sounding genuinely incensed. "Not that it will help speed my death any, but if it's any consolation..." He lowered his tone. "That really hurt."

Gushing blood from Malaya's ruined shoulder spattered onto Cyan.

"Watch where you bleed," said Cyan. "You're getting that on me."

"Oh, I am, am I?" Malaya's body pointed his neck in Cyan's direction. Something like a muffled wet cough emerged from the neck, showering Cyan from head to toe in blood.

"Stop that," said Cyan, and cupped his eyes with his hands. It was bad enough that the smell was nauseating. The dragon's thick blood had blinded him.

"Or else what?"

Cyan growled, then voiced a full-fledged scream. "I'm going to cut you to pieces!"

Before he could move, the dragon thrust his own head at Cyan with his one good claw and bit down. Teeth clenched, the dragon yanked his claw back, ripping Cyan in half—his torso still in his jaws and the legs and waist lying where the man once stood. He promptly spat the man's limp body back out.

* * *

As Cyan lay dead, Malaya collected his body parts and put himself back together. New flesh sprouted to join the severed parts to his body.

Suddenly the dead man leapt to his feet—intact, strangely enough—ax in hand to do battle once more. This time, however, Malaya was ready for him. He let loose a blast of fire from his mouth that left nothing but charred bones where the man once stood.

* * *

The dragon watched, curious, as the blackened bones knit and layer upon layer of flesh covered them. Before long Cyan was whole and on his feet, clenching his teeth in frenzied anger. His eyebrows angled downward sharply as his face contorted into a hateful sneer, while the veins in his neck showed visibly beneath his skin.

Cyan stood in a half crouch, his knees hunched forward for a moment before rushing toward the dragon, brandishing his heavy ax with one hand. He had lost the look of a rational creature.

Not wanting to kill him again for fear that he'd only have to do so over and over, Malaya commanded a wall of earth to rise up from the ground and divide the chamber between him and Cyan. Cyan pounded against the wall with his ax, but upon noticing that he wasn't accomplishing anything, he turned his efforts toward scaling the wall instead. He leapt up and grasped the top of the wall with both hands, kicking against it with his feet to propel him upward.

Malaya made the wall rise to double its original height. The sudden surge shook Cyan off and he landed on his back. He leapt to his feet and began anew.

With both hands he swung his ax above his head and brought it down onto the top of the wall, anchoring it in place in the packed soil. Using the blade of the ax as a makeshift grappling hook he clambered up the wall once more, pulling himself up by the handle of his weapon, but when he reached the top Malaya let the wall collapse onto Cyan, covering him up to his neck in soil. The soil immediately hardened into solid stone that held him tight.

"That will teach you not to mess with me," said Malaya.

"Let me out of here!" yelled Cyan.

"Why?"

"So I can gut you like a deer! That's why!"

"Wrong answer," Malaya responded, his green scales beginning to turn brown like the soil in order to return to it.

"Wait," Cyan said in a new tone of voice. It didn't sound quite so much pathetic as it did conniving.

"Yes?"

"You're... you're not going to leave me here are you?"

"I just might. If you pose a threat to the medal of earth and I cannot vanquish you, then the only alternative I have left is to imprison you forever."

Cyan swallowed hard. Eternal life didn't sound quite so good anymore. "Please let me go."

"No."

"Please! I promise I won't hurt you anymore! Please don't let me stay like this forever!"

The dragon remained silent for a short while, contemplating what he should do. Those brief moments seemed like an eternity to Cyan.

"No," said Malaya.

That remark nearly caused Cyan to break into tears. How ironic it was that one who could not die would be sentenced to a fate worse than death, an eternity of confinement and isolation from the outside world.

"You can't leave me here!" Cyan yelled, and it was little more than a forceful whine.

"Oh I can't, can I? Tell me if you still think that after a few millennia."

"That's inhuman!"

"I'm not human."

"That's... that's cruel and unusual punishment!"

"So sue me."

Cyan's lip quivered. "Ple-e-e-e-ease don't leave me here!" he bawled.

"Oh, all right," said Malaya, at his wit's end. "Have it your way then. What with all your whining, I'll never get any sleep." The dragon slapped the mound of earth with his tail and the rock instantly became soft sand. As the dirt streamed off Cyan he fell over, landing on his face.

"Now get out of here," Malaya commanded. "Do not make the mistake of returning, ever."

The dragon's scales quickly turned earthy-brown and his body became as the soil before sinking into the ground beneath his feet.

What a mess I've made of things, Cyan thought, realizing his mistake. Without the medal of earth he would never rid himself of the blessing-turned-curse of immortality. And it frightened him to think what the dragon would do to him if he dared show his face in the shrine again.

"Are you still here?" Malaya's voice echoed throughout the chamber, though he was nowhere to be seen.

"I'm leaving now," he blurted, his words stumbling over one another in their haste to get out. He gripped his wind charm and the green gale lifted him off his feet, making his body lighter than air for a split second before disappearing in a flash of green.

V

Cyan had blinked as the green light engulfed him. His eyes opened in time to see he was falling into a sand dune. He hit the dune face first, burying him up to his waist with his legs stuck up in the air, looking like a tossed javelin.

He pulled himself out of the dune and looked around. To his left and right lay a seemingly interminable stretch of beach. Ahead of him was the ocean, its foam-crowned waters lapping at his feet. He turned in place. Behind him was a small town just beyond the reach of the white sands, its tallest building peeking out over a hill of healthy grass.

His ears perked to a whistling sound, very strong now but previously weak and drowned out by the crashing of the waves. He looked skyward. His ax plummeted out of the sky, twirling in the air as it descended onto him, splitting him in half.

* * *

"R-r-r-r-r-a-a-a-a-a-a-a!" screamed Cyan, starting first with a growl. The warrior bellowed like an injured animal. He flailed against the beach, angry at no one in particular, but needing to vent his rage regardless. He tore away handfuls of sand at a time, kicked at the dunes, hurled his body against them, kicking, biting, screaming. A startled crab clambered out of its burrow in the sand. Cyan, spying it, immediately leapt up and crushed its shell under his heel, grinding it down with repeated stomps before pitching headfirst into the dunes once more.

He raged on until he was completely spent. Cyan tried to stand but couldn't. He felt more exhausted than he could ever remember. His vision dimmed, then all went black.

When finally he came to his senses, he was lying on a stiff cot. For a moment he thought he was still campaigning.

A young woman strode into the room.

"Good morning," she said. "Feeling better?"

"I feel… fine," he said, perplexed. He wasn't sure what she meant by this question. What had happened to him that she should be asking that, and who was she, and how did he get here?

"You gave us quite a scare yesterday," she continued. "We found you unconscious at the shore and thought we'd arrived too late."

"Where am I?"

She shot him a strange look.

"Have I offended you somehow?" he asked.

"Marginally," she said, her look melting into a sort of coy half smile. "What way is that to thank your rescuer?"

Remembering his manners, he bowed and kissed her hand. "My name is Cyan Wraithwate of Nordon. Thank you for your hospitality."

"You are quite welcome," the girl responded. "I'm Eleanor."

"Please tell me where I am."

Eleanor rocked back slightly. "First tell me how you got here."

Cyan gritted his teeth. It wouldn't do to have her know the true reason for his coming.

"I…" he stammered. "I am a sailor. From abroad. We—we got caught in a storm, and our boat sank." He did his best to look mournful. "I think everyone else drowned."

"But you?"

"Yes," he said flatly.

"You must be a strong swimmer."

Cyan nodded.

Eleanor crossed her arms. "Especially if you made it here wearing all that armor."

His heart sank just like the imaginary ship in his story when she saw through his lies. But this feeling was nothing compared to the shock that was yet to come. The bracer had claimed more of his body—his left leg from his thigh to his ankle was lifeless iron.

Cyan let out a panicked shriek and clasped his hands to his face.

Eleanor pushed him. "I saved your life—why would you lie to me?"

His jaw dropped. Cyan was as flabbergasted at having been caught in a lie as he was with this girl laying hands on him.

"Get out," Eleanor said.

"No, wait…"

"I said, out!" she yelled, shoving him out the door to the room.

Cyan clamped onto to the doorframe and dug his heels into the floor. "I need help. You have to help me!"

"You're a liar is what you are, and I'll have nothing to do with you."

She rammed her shoulder into the small of his back, sending him headfirst to the floor. He spun over and sat up, backing away from her.

"I'll admit, you have no reason to believe me," he said. "But at least hear me out. This time I swear I'll tell the truth."

She sighed. "Make it quick, I'm busy."

"A curse was put on me. The armor I'm wearing won't come off. It's eating me up like a disease."

"A likely story."

"Look, this piece here," he said, pointing to the bracer. "See? No fasteners." He tugged at it. "It won't come off. None of it does."

"You're lying."

"You can keep it if you can take it off me," said Cyan. He stood. "You'd be doing me a favor."

Eleanor kept silent, her steely eyes pinned on Cyan.

"Could you please tell me where I am?" he asked.

"You are in our village of Aranoa."

Cyan shook his head. "Am I anywhere near the water dragon's home?"

Her eyebrows pitched down sharply. "I'll not have that kind of talk."

"What? What did I do now?"

"You speak blasphemies."

Palms up, he shrugged. "How am I supposed to know…"

Her dour eyes stopped him cold.

"I must speak to it," said Cyan, changing the subject.

39

"Her," she corrected. "And you can go pray to her when…"

"No, I mean, I have to see her."

Eleanor chortled. "Good luck with that. No one sees here."

"Why?"

She gave an exasperated sigh at having to explain the obvious. "Because she lives at the bottom of the ocean."

Cyan's head drooped to his chest, his shoulders caved with the hopelessness of his mission. He knit his fingers behind his head and paced away, giving his back to her.

"Why are you so interested in seeing our patroness?" she asked.

"Only she can raise the curse that afflicts me," he said, looking down at his feet.

Eleanor uncrossed her arms. Cyan must have made for a pitiable sight. "We have no means of visiting our patroness," she said. "I'm sorry."

"No, you're not," Cyan muttered. "You don't understand."

"You think you have problems?" She grabbed his shoulder and spun him around to face her. "Here I am minding an empty shop while father's breaking his back at his anvil. You…" she trailed off. "You have some nerve. The sooner I'm rid of you, the better."

She shoved him dead-center in the chest and Cyan stumbled backward a few steps. He caught her arms by the elbows when she went to do it again.

"Leave," she said, thrashing against him. "You're not welcome here."

"Calm down," said Cyan. "I need your help."

"I've helped you enough as it is," she said, wrenching an arm free of his grip.

"Just… just…" Cyan let her go and backed away slowly. "I'll go. Just please, show me where the water dragon lives."

Eleanor, her face still red with anger, remained silent. "Fine," she said, and tramped out the door.

VI

She led him down to the beach where she found him. The tide had partially washed away the imprint he had left in the sand when he landed.

"Here we are," she said.

Cyan cupped his eyes and scanned the horizon, then either side of the beach. "Where?"

"Out there," she replied, pointing toward the water. "The shrine is just offshore. And underwater," she said testily. "You can't see it where you stand now, but from the deck of a ship you can, if you look straight down into the water."

Cyan turned to face her.

"Don't let that fool you," she went on. "It's further down than you can swim, and strong currents from below push you back to the surface if you try. You'd need gills to swim down there."

He turned back to look into the horizon. It was hopeless. It was bad enough that he had failed to get one dragon's medal when he needed them all. It was insult to injury that getting the next one was impossible. He took a long breath and let it out in a sigh that caved his shoulders.

"Take me back," he said, wheeling around to face Eleanor. She was gone, presumably already on the way back to her store. "Damn it," he murmured.

Cyan plodded into the water until he was ankle-deep. He stopped, immediately rethinking his actions. Gritting his teeth, Cyan high-stepped into the waves.

The seafloor ramped downward quickly into a sheer cliff wall. Ahead and several dozen feet below him, the domed peak of the water shrine rose up from a flat patch of seabed at the bottom of the defile. He hesitated at the edge. His lungs had begun to ache—if he turned back now, he figured he could make it to open air again. Cyan clenched his eyes shut and leapt into to crevasse. His armor dragged him down toward the bottom with little effort on his part.

He was not halfway down when a current billowed up from below, halting his downward progress. He rotated dead-down and pulled against the current, but could not make headway. A violent push from beneath launched him bodily out of the water and back onto the shallows. He lay there, dazed.

Cyan sat up in waist-high water. He could feel his cheeks flushing with fresh anger. He stood and kicked at the next wave, then turned to head back to town.

Going solely by memory, Cyan made his way back to Eleanor's shop. She sat behind the counter, tending to an otherwise empty shop. When she saw him her eyebrows pitched down sharply.

"Didn't I tell you…"

"I need to see your father," he cut her off.

"He's busy."

"I don't care. Take me to him."

"He won't…"

"Do as I say!" he shouted over her.

Her cheeks were plum red. Without another word, she rounded the counter and bade for him to follow.

She led him outside and around the shop to an adjoining walkway. The path led behind the store to an old workshop. The building had seen many seasons of patchwork repair. As Eleanor pushed open the door, a blast of heat rippled Cyan's vision. He rubbed his eyes and stepped in.

The orange glow from the forge at the end of the workshop cast long shadows across the room. Cyan sidled past swords and armor on racks that were but outlines in the stark lighting. With the heat and the ear-splitting peal of hammered metal, Cyan hoped his meeting with the smith would be short.

At the far end of the room, the blacksmith hammered a mass of iron on his anvil. The smith was huge—a man as broad as he was tall, and he stood

45

easily as tall as Cyan. His bald head and crown of white hair spoke to his age. The glowing blaze cast his body in orange, red and black. He worked oblivious to his two customers, so engrossed was he in his work.

"Father," Eleanor said, trying to get the smith's attention. "Father!"

The smith halted partway into raising his hammer. He looked over his shoulder and set his tools down, then turned to address Eleanor.

The man wiped his brow with a meaty forearm. The man's face was caked with soot. "Yes?"

Cyan stepped forward before Eleanor could introduce him. "I am Cyan Wraithwate," he said, frigidly cordial as he extended his hand.

"Horatio," the smith answered, his tone gravelly. He gave a firm handshake and nearly dislocated Cyan's shoulder. "What do you want?"

"I've come to discuss business."

Horatio glanced at Eleanor with narrowed eyes. "Eleanor tends the store," he said in a heavy tone to drive the point home.

She crossed her arms and glowered at her father before shifting her gaze to Cyan.

Without another word, Horatio turned back to his anvil.

"We misunderstood each other," Cyan said. "I want something not in your store."

"Nothing in here is for sale."

"I need you to make something."

Horatio set his hand on his hammer, hesitated before picking it up. "What have you got in mind?"

Cyan smiled, knowing then he'd piqued the man's interest. "I need a helmet..."

"Bloody hell!" Horatio wheeled back around. "You wasted my time for this?"

"It's not just any helmet." He paused for effect. "It's a diving helmet."

Horatio laughed. "You're daft. Going for a swim with a helmet made of metal?"

"Can you make one or not?" Cyan spoke over him.

The blacksmith sauntered over until he was inches from Cyan. He crossed his arms. "I can make anything. You just tell me how you want it. What's in it for me?"

A wicked grin curled Cyan's lips. He spread his arms. "You can have my armor."

"I'm convinced you're daft. You'd trade a near full suit of armor for just a helmet, and then you'd use that helmet to take a dip in the ocean." Horatio gave a belly-shaking laugh. "Oh, that's rich. Just don't come crying if your helmet sinks you straight to the bottom."

"Sir," Cyan said with deadpan stillness, "that is what I expect it to do."

Eleanor stood agape. "That's suicide."

"None of your concern," said Cyan, glancing at her. He turned back to Horatio. "I'll also need weighted boots to make sure I get to the bottom."

"Supposing I go through with this," Horatio said, "and you sink to the bottom, how am I supposed to retrieve your armor as payment?"

"Simple," Cyan replied on a rush of insight. "Tie a rope around my waist and tether the other end to the beach. Then just reel me in after an hour or two."

Eleanor leveled a hard look on Cyan. "That's ghoulish. I won't have a man's blood on my hands."

"You won't," said Cyan, with an irony only he could appreciate. "Nor will your father. I'll tell you what—after I've tethered myself down, you can come along an hour later and discover my body. You'll not witness anything, and I won't tell anybody because I'll be dead." Cyan fought the urge to smile at his cleverness.

Horatio cradled his chin in a massive hand.

"Father!" Eleanor chastised. "You're not actually considering this, are you?"

"What is there to consider?" Cyan spoke up. "I can tell by your father's face that we have a bargain."

Horatio snorted hard out his nose, then gave a single, solemn nod.

VII

Sunup the following morning found Cyan again at the beach. Trailing behind him was Horatio, who still wasn't convinced that Cyan was so intent on drowning himself and had come along to watch Cyan back out at the last minute. In the event he was wrong, he'd be there to collect his due sooner. It worked out either way.

Cyan sat down on the sand. Horatio sidled up to him and handed him four rough ingots of black iron. Cyan tied these two of each to his thighs, then reached for the helmet.

"I'll bet you a day's wages you'll thrash up to the surface once you're out of breath," said Horatio.

Cyan paused partway to donning the helmet. "Were I worried about running out of air, I would have asked you to cut breathing holes into this helmet."

Horatio gave an earnest nod, as Cyan had a point.

Cyan dropped the helmet onto his head. It was a snug fit, especially with the modifications at its front to accommodate a thick pane of glass as a viewing window.

"Let's not forget this, now," said Horatio, holding up a rope tied in a lasso. He slipped it over Cyan's head and tightened it around his waist.

With Horatio's help, Cyan stood up. His knees buckled with the added weight. One ponderous step at a time, he waddled to the shore and into the water. Once he was waist-deep, he snatched a clump of shop towels from his pocket and jammed them into the opening between his neck and the helmet's lower rim. He took one final breath before stopping the helmet up completely and plunging beneath the waves.

Cyan reached the underwater precipice and leapt. Down, down, down, he sank, sped on by the weight of his diving gear. Water trickled into the seam between the towels and the helmet—it wasn't airtight, but it didn't matter, ultimately.

A sharp snag halted him in mid-fall and he bent over at his middle. The rope was stretched taut above him. He reached behind his back for his ax and hacked through the rope. It gave with a sudden jerk, as no doubt Horatio—who'd been holding on to it the whole time—had probably toppled onto his backside when the pull from Cyan's end went slack. Cyan smirked.

Bent over as he was, his body rotated head down from the weight of his helmet as his descent began anew. His progress slowed as he neared the seafloor.

Strong currents from beneath whipped up to push him back up to the surface just as before. This time, his added weight overpowered the currents. He missed his mark and landed headfirst into a seaweed patch at the outskirts of the shrine, burying himself in the soil up to his waist. He was stuck fast.

Knowing he didn't have much time before he was out of air, he clawed at the muck. With a mighty heave he tore his arms free and grabbed a handful of seaweed, pulling at the grass to yank himself out of the seafloor.

Cyan righted himself and the slurry of water and sand in his helmet settled just beneath his nose. He hauled himself through the seaweed at a painfully slow pace. Every once in a while they broke, pitching him headlong into the muck. He struggled to move forward, pulling with one arm then the other, even as his lungs burned for air.

He coughed, then again, and then all his air left him in one forceful rush. His stomach and lungs flooded with water. There was an instant of panic, then darkness, then, for only a short while, the feeling that he was sinking, until that too was gone.

* * *

Anger exploded in him as the bracer's magic took hold. His stomach heaved and emptied the water it held into his helmet. Arm over arm Cyan pulled himself along, faster than before. Mere seconds later, his body failed him once again. Deprived of an air supply, it was not long before Cyan's consciousness faded altogether.

* * *

New life coursed through Cyan once more as his body kicked on with a jolt. He hauled himself the rest of the way through the seaweed and set foot on the water shrine's stone portico. Before he could run out of air again, he leap through the shrine's door. His body coasted through the water then suddenly dropped to the floor. Somehow, inexplicably, he had leapt through to open air inside the shrine.

He clawed away the shop towels keeping his helmet (mostly) watertight. A torrent of slurry poured out of his helmet. His lungs still burning, he shoved the helmet off of him and collapsed to his knees. He coughed out seawater for a long time.

Cyan vowed never to take breathable air for granted again.

He stood and readied his ax, holding it in both hands as he looked around. This shrine was very similar to the last one he'd traveled to. Stained glass windows built into the walls on either side portrayed the same pictures seen in the earth temple. He wondered how such large windows could hold up against the force of the tides. Strange forces had to be at work here; panes of glass as large as these could never endure the constant buffeting of the ocean.

It wasn't completely dark inside, thanks to the light coming in through the windows. Small, irregularly shaped blue tiles on the walls glimmered in the dim sunlight. They formed a mural of waves crashing at sea. The floor was covered with these same tiles but in a spiral pattern of alternating light and dark blues.

At the end of the path stood a heavy chamber door reinforced with iron beams. On either side of the doorway were statues of a hideous half-man, half-fish creature. Each held a three-pronged trident in its powerful grip and stood at attention at the door.

Cyan rapped loudly on the door with his knuckles then stepped back, half expecting those statues to come to life. Nothing happened. He approached the door again and pulled it open.

He was immediately taken aback. A ring of water circumscribed the interior of the chamber, all the way up to the ceiling. Fish of all sorts swam unafraid in the ring of water, sharing the space with sharks and dolphins. Once the path was clear, he pushed through the water and back into the open air in the heart of the shrine.

"Dragon," he called out, "if you are here, show yourself!"

No sooner had he spoken than a pair of bright green eyes opened in the water across from where he stood. Then a shape began to appear around the eyes; first an outline, then a translucent image of a huge blue dragon with her tail curled around her body. She slinked out of the water and into the center of the shrine.

She was dark blue and smooth skinned, not scaled like the previous dragon he had encountered. Not a bead of water remained on her body, as though the water and she were one and the same.

"Welcome," she said. "Although I can't begin to guess how you made it here, it is nice that you would pay me a visit."

A dolphin cried out from the water.

"Just a second." The blue dragon turned around to face the dolphin. It floated in place, waiting to be acknowledged.

"Okay, come here," she said to it, rearing up on her hind legs.

Cyan gawked. On all fours, the dragoness was huge in her own right, but standing erect, she was enormous. If he hadn't learned his lesson before, Cyan now knew better than ever that these creatures were not to be trifled with.

The dolphin leapt out of the wall of water and into her waiting arms. It squeaked its delight as she cuddled it. Then, turning back toward him, the dragoness said, "Sorry about that. He's the clingy sort."

"Don't dolphins need water to survive?" asked Cyan, who was having quite a time trying to make any sense of anything.

"Yes," she replied. "But the medal of water sustains him here in my home. With it I maintain harmony in the oceans and balance in the tides." She paused for a moment and whispered something to the dolphin, and they both laughed quietly to themselves. "What brings you here?" she asked.

Cyan opened his mouth to speak but just as quickly stopped himself to give his response some thought. If he didn't answer satisfactorily he would be out two elemental treasures, and lacking even one he would never raise his curse. For all his efforts, no reasonable answer came to mind.

"Not much of a conversationalist, are you?" the dragoness asked. "Maybe we should begin with our names. I am Imhra." Her gaze held steady on the ax Cyan held in his hands. "You won't be using that to chop wood down here, now will you?"

Cyan swallowed hard in a dry throat.

"That ax is meant for me, isn't it?" she said, sounding more hurt than afraid.

"No," said Cyan, setting down his ax.

"Then why did you bring it?"

"I mean," Cyan stammered, "it was meant for you, but I've decided against that."

"You came down here to kill me?" she said, wide-eyed. "Fair warning: I can't die."

"Well that makes two of us," Cyan muttered.

"How do you mean that?"

Cyan took a sharp breath on realizing she'd heard him. "I... I mean..." He sighed. "There's no harm in telling you. I've come for the medal of water."

"You didn't answer my question," she said sharply. "Regardless, what do you want with it?"

"I am a cursed man. This armor I wear takes more of me each day, turning my skin into lifeless iron. I cannot remove any of it until the curse is broken, and that can only happen when I have acquired all of the elemental treasures."

She nodded. "And you decided to come to me first?"

"No, I visited the earth dragon..."

"Malaya."

"Yes."

She smiled. "I haven't seen him in so long. Did he give you his medal?"

"No," Cyan answered, mildly embarrassed. "We did not hit it off quite as well as I would have hoped."

"You cut off his head, didn't you?"

"Y-yes," Cyan answered, put off by her suddenness.

"Oh, he doesn't like that. That's the fastest way to get on his nerves. If you had just asked him politely, he might have given it to you on the condition that you'd bring it back when you're done with it."

Cyan looked down at his feet. "May I please have the medal of water?"

"No."

He groaned. It was worth a try.

"You have a dark past, Cyan Wraithwate," she said. "I read it in your face. You've done a lot of bad things."

Cyan lowered his head. He was as good as done for. He though on interesting poses to assume when his end finally came and he'd be frozen in place, encased in iron. With any luck he'd be discovered and installed as a statue in a town plaza, and not pawned off as scrap iron or worse—found by Horatio and melted down to make horseshoes.

"But," she said, after a beat, "I believe in second chances. Do you?"

"No," the answer was wrung from him. It surprised him even that he'd said it.

"I can't just give you the medal," she went on. "But I'll give you a fair shot at earning it. Along with all the bad you've done, I also see a willingness to repent."

Hope surged anew in his breast. "What would you have me do?"

"Nothing short of defeating me."

He scowled. "Now you're just toying with me. I can't defeat you—you don't die!"

"I didn't say you had to kill me." She held up a talon to make her point. "Just put up a good fight."

"Can't I fight your shrine guardian instead?"

"You mean those stone statues outside my chamber?"

"Yes."

She rolled her eyes. "I was being facetious. They're just stone statues." She extended her arms into the wall of water and the dolphin swam happily away. "I did hear you correctly when you said you can't die, correct?"

Cyan choked up on his weapon. "Yes."

She dropped to all fours. "I find that amusing."

He was not sure what she meant by that, but the connotation spoke of all sorts of harm that might come his way.

"I did too, for a while," he said. "It got old quickly."

"Well," she said, lowering her head until it was level with Cyan's face. She smiled, revealing twin rows of vicious fangs. "Let's get started, shall we?"

She snapped at him, narrowly missing his head. Cyan leapt back and tumbled onto his backside, somersaulted over. He scrambled to his feet not a moment too soon, as she reared up and brought her forelimbs down hard, pounding the floor where he had stood only a moment ago.

Cyan wheeled away from her as she tramped forward, her jaws snapping in the air between them. Biting cold water prickled the skin on his shoulder and he stopped. Behind him was the wall of water. If he kept this up, she would force him into the water and he would drown. Again.

Faced with no other alternatives, Cyan hefted his ax and swung it for the base of her neck. Her left forearm darted up to fend off the blow. Cyan's steel rang on contact. The impact sent painful tremors up his arms and he let go of his ax. No sooner had he realized his mistake than he sent his gaze flying up to Imhra. His ax was stuck in her forearm, which she had fast-frozen into solid ice. She worked the ax out of her arm and tossed it carelessly over her shoulder. A wicked grin spread across her face.

Cyan hardly had time to scream as she descended upon him with her jaws. She bit down and gave him a vicious shake before flinging him across the shrine. His body collapsed in a mangled heap on the other side, but Cyan was dead even before then.

* * *

Cyan's eyelids flew open and all he saw was red. He clawed on all fours to his ax and gnashed his teeth at Imhra.

"That's one point for me," she said.

Water seeped out of the wall surrounding them and covered the floor in a shallow pond.

Screaming like an injured animal, Cyan charged her with his ax at the ready. Just as he got within striking distance, the ground sprouted icicles the size of lances. Cyan's mad rush came to an abrupt halt on impaling himself upon a mass of icicles. His body slumped forward. With the last of his waning strength, he hefted his ax up over his head on the off chance he might score a blow. His intentions were telegraphed a long way off. With but a glance, Imhra instantly melted the icicles. Cyan collapsed onto his face, oozing blood from the puckering wounds that mottled his torso and thighs.

"Two to nothing," were the last words Cyan heard her say as everything went black.

* * *

Cyan snapped awake and thrashed, finding that he could not move any part of his body beneath his neck. He was encased from the shoulders down in a block of solid ice. If he weren't already furious at having been killed, he was more so for having been bound down.

"Care to try again?" Imhra said, backing herself against the wall of water. A forest of icicles sprouted up from the ground in a semicircle around her. Then the air in the shrine grew humid. Before long a heavy raincloud had formed in the air above their heads.

"Let's see you get out of this," she said as the rain started to fall.

Cyan bucked against the ice, at first shifting it, then getting it to rock back and forth in a steady rhythm until it toppled over. It shattered on impact, spilling him facedown on the floor.

He clawed to his feet, snatched up his ax in midstride and charged Imhra's wall of icicles. He brought his ax down onto the ice with the full weight of his body, lopping the heads off of several at once.

Over and over he hefted his ax, making little headway for all his effort. Meanwhile the raindrops were coming faster—his calves were below water.

Imhra shifted position behind her barrier. She lay down and propped her head up on her elbows to watch Cyan. "I find I sleep better when it rains," she said. "The constant drumming is soothing, don't you think?"

"Shut up!"

Imhra pantomimed taking offense. "Strange way to die, isn't it? Drowning, I mean. I can't imagine what that must be like."

Cyan gritted his teeth and focused on his work. He buried his ax up to its shaft in an icicle. Planting his foot against the ice he wrenched the blade free, only to lose his balance and tumble backward into the water.

He stood up, and the water was at his waist. If it rose any more his arms would be under the surface and he would not be able to swing his ax with any force. He hacked at the wall at double speed now, ice chips trailing the path of his ax through the air. It wasn't long before he was winded. He set his ax down and slumped against its grip.

"Giving up already?" Imhra asked from behind the row of icicles. Although he could not see all of her between the gaps in the ice, he knew she was gloating.

She had won. The water level rose above his shoulders. Waves lapped at his chin. He'd never breach the wall of ice now.

Just then he had an idea. He bent his knees, submerging himself completely. Then, like a spring released from compression, he pushed off the bottom, leaping up and forward through the water with his ax in the lead. He snaked headlong through gaps between the icicles, his body resting on their sides. In his grip, in one hand, was his ax, its blade inches short of Imhra's snout.

Imhra eased away from the honed edge. "We can allow you one point for that," she said.

The raincloud dissipated back into the wall of water, draining the chamber floor dry. The icicles receded and Cyan dropped to the floor.

"Not bad," Imhra acknowledged.

Cyan doubled over onto all fours and coughed seawater out of his lungs. "That... wasn't... fun..." he stammered, and then doubled over and coughed out more water.

"It was for me."

"May I..." he cut off, cupped his mouth with his hand and coughed. "May I have your medal now?"

"No."

Cyan's eyes grew wide.

"Where's the surprise in that?" she asked. "You didn't actually defeat me. But what I can do is offer a rematch. Next time, you fight me without the use of your weapon."

"That's not fair!" Cyan yelled, getting to his feet.

"Do you want the medal of water or not?"

"Yes," he said, grudgingly.

"Good. Then you'll do as I say." She plodded up alongside him. "We need something to make this next fight more interesting. Maybe…" she trailed off. "Maybe if you were to get Malaya's earth medal, you'd be able to put up a more entertaining fight."

"He won't give it to me," replied Cyan.

"He might if you tell him I sent you." She raised a claw and a globe of water rose up from her palm. The water condensed into a dark blue stone disk. Inscribed in its center was a symbol resembling the ocean at a moderate chop.

"Take this," she said, handing him the stone. "Show it to him. Once he knows you have my support, I'm sure he'll trust you with the earth medal."

Cyan put the stone in his pocket, saying, "But the last time I confronted him he trapped me in the ground, saying that he would never let me go. He said never to return to his shrine, or else he'd do something worse."

"He wouldn't hurt you if you returned to apologize. Malaya can be stern at times, but he isn't heartless."

He considered her advice. Returning to the shrine of the earth dragon could have two results: he would retrieve the medal of earth and use it to defeat the water dragon, in which case he would be halfway rid of his curse; or, the earth dragon might still be angry with him, and upon seeing the warrior again he would not be so lenient. It was an all-or-nothing situation, and a risk he had to take.

"Have you decided?" she asked.

He nodded. "If I'm not back shortly, I'm probably forever buried in the ground," he said with a half-grin.

Invoking the wind charm, he spoke his destination. As the green winds swirled around him he shut his eyes before the flash of light could blind him.

VIII

Cyan's landing was less than smooth. Face-first he fell onto the doorstep of the earth shrine. Blood streamed from his nose—he had broken it, he was sure. He pinched the bridge of his nose with his knuckles and gave it a twist, and the pain was enough to ripple his vision. He sat on the shrine's front stoop to settle himself as the pain subsided.

He stood up and planted a hand against the wall for support. Nose pinched to stop the bleeding, he tilted his head back and suddenly his ax came into view above him, plowing through the overhanging tree branches. Screaming, Cyan hurled himself through the doors of the shrine, taking cover under its stone roof as a loud "clang!" pealed from outside.

Stepping back outside, he could see no trace of his ax. He looked up again and saw why—the ax had struck the roof covering the entryway and had embedded itself in the stone, its handle jutting out horizontally toward the forest. Positioning himself under the handle of his ax he raised his palms, then leapt up to knock the weapon free of the stone. After four hits the ax jerked free of the rock and fell to the forest floor, and Cyan, now with ax in hand, re-entered the earth shrine.

Lupine stalked the dark recesses of the shrine. All that Cyan saw of him was his glowing yellow eyes. Lupine had been expecting for him.

"You return?" he asked, not quite surprised. "The master said you would."

"I come in peace," said Cyan.

Lupine crossed his arms. "A likely story."

"I need to speak to the dragon…"

"I cannot allow that," the wolfman interrupted.

Cyan made for the door and Lupine shoved him back.

"I am under orders to end your life if you persist," said Lupine.

"I dare you to try."

Snarling, Lupine drew his sword. The wolfman advanced with a forehand swing. Cyan parried with the shaft of his ax, catching Lupine's weapon in the crook of his own. Cyan tugged, wresting the sword free of Lupine's grip. The blow set Lupine off balance. Cyan wasted no time in planting a foot on the startled wolfman's chest and giving a fierce shove, sending Lupine to the ground.

Lupine rolled over and crawled to his sword. Cyan kicked it away.

"You are no position to bargain now," said Cyan, his ax blade hovering inches from Lupine's throat.

"Let me through to the earth dragon or I will kill you."

"Such threats, little man," Lupine said. He gave a single hacking laugh that sounded too much like a bark for Cyan's liking. He rolled onto his back and put his hands up in surrender.

Cyan raised his weapon, and only then realized his mistake.

Lupine's clenched fist ignited like a brilliant green star. Cyan was instantly hurled backward against the far wall. He was stuck fast to it about a foot off the ground, unable to move at all.

Lupine sprinted up to him on all fours and stopped right before the warrior. "As a servant of the guardian of the earth shrine, I too share in his power," Lupine spoke into his face. Wads of spittle flew from the wolfman's slavering jaws with each word.

"Behold," he went on, "your very armor betrays you. The metal you wear is held to the wall by magnetic forces at my command."

Cyan tried to speak but his jaw, much like the rest of his body, refused to move.

"As if that was not enough," Lupine said, "your blood is high in iron too." He gave another barking laugh. "Let's see how much blood is in you."

An inner pull fought the current of Cyan's blood. All at once the color drained from his field of vision.

Drowsiness set in as blood flowed away from his head.

"If you can still hear me," said Lupine, "know that I will make your death quick."

Lupine shut his eyes and concentrated. In rough jerks Cyan's blood was siphoned out of the periphery his body, turning him deathly pale. The blood converged at his midsection. His body swelled at his chest, gorged with blood.

Lupine extended his hands and brought them closer to himself, palms turned inward as though gesturing for someone to follow. Meanwhile Cyan's midsection bent forward, in the direction of the wolfman.

All at once his organs burst from within, the sudden shock snapping his ribcage. Neck to navel Cyan opened like a filleted fish, the explosion dousing Lupine in his blood. Cyan collapsed in a heap of ragged flesh and splintered bone. Lupine sat, content, and licked the viscera from his arms.

* * *

Cyan awoke to new life with smoldering anger in his heart and the desire to make Lupine nothing more than just a memory and a runny smear on the ground. He snatched up his ax and leapt to his feet, braying like a wild animal.

Lupine gave a start and looked over his shoulder. "What manner of demon are you?"

Cyan closed on Lupine in bounding steps. He sprang forward on the balls of his feet and tackled the wolfman, landing atop him with the shaft of his ax against Lupine's neck.

"Open. That. Door," Cyan spat the words out through clenched teeth. His body surged. It took all the force of his will to rein himself in. Rage pounded a steady beat—he felt it in his bones, his blood, his skin. His mind raced, consumed with thoughts of how easily he could kill Lupine. A quick shove and he'd snap his neck against the shaft of his ax.

Lupine nodded that he would comply.

Cyan clenched his eyes shut. "Go. Now," he said, fighting the compulsion. He leapt off of Lupine and lay flat on his back, waiting for the sensation to pass.

Lupine stood and shot Cyan a wary glance before turning to the door and hauling it open.

It was a long string of moments before Cyan could trust himself not to kill Lupine. He rolled over onto his chest, then brought his legs up under him and stood. Lupine said nothing as Cyan walked into the inner sanctuary, but the wolfman's low growl said more than any words could.

Cyan found the chamber empty, just as before. "Hello?"

The ground shook as the earth dragon roused from his sleep, taking shape from beneath a mound of dirt. He opened his eyes and leveled a disdainful look at Cyan once the soil had run down his scales completely.

"Mr. Wraithwate," said Malaya, "I am dismayed to see you again, and only because now I'll have to make good on my threat."

Cyan swallowed hard. "Wait! I've not come for the medal, if that's what you're thinking." He let his ax fall from his hand. "I come in peace."

"Do tell — why?"

"Because," Cyan trailed off. He could kick himself for how stupid he looked now. "I want to apologize," he murmured, making sure not to look Malaya in the eyes.

"Oh really?" Malaya asked, sounding so surprised as to border on sardonic. "What for?"

Cyan groaned. "What I did to you was impolite and harmful."

"You mean all that decapitation and dismemberment business?"

"Yes," he blurted.

Malaya took a pause. "What else do you have to say?"

"That is all."

"Good." Malaya paced away. "I accept your apology. In the grander scheme of things, you didn't cause any harm, I suppose." He turned to face Cyan. "You will be leaving now?"

"No..."

Malaya's eyes narrowed. His lips drew back to reveal a glint of fang. "What is it you want?" he asked, but by his tone, the question was rhetorical.

Cyan sighed. "I've come again for the medal of earth."

"You can't have it. You, Cyan, are as insensitive, malicious, and evil a soul as they come." He paused to consider the point. "Do you even have a soul, Cyan? Because I have my doubts."

"Don't do this to me." Cyan fell to his knees. "I know I don't deserve your generosity, but unless you give me your medal, I'm doomed."

"Much as it pains me to say this, I am afraid I can do nothing for you."

"I can change!" Cyan nearly cut him off. "I can... I can become a better person. All I need is for you to give me the chance."

Malaya shook his head.

"If one of your peers were to put her faith in me, would that be reason enough for you to trust me with your medal?" asked Cyan, showing him the stone Imhra had given him.

Malaya's eyes widened when he saw it. "That is the sea dragon's," he said, thunderstruck. "How did you get that?"

"She gave it to me and told me to show it to you."

He remained silent for a long while. "Imhra gave this to you freely and told you to show it to me?"

"Yes," Cyan responded, putting the stone away.

The dragon remained silent, locked in deep thought. "If she trusts you, then perhaps I can as well," he said at last.

Cyan's heart leapt.

Malaya commanded a narrow pillar of earth to rise from the ground to his left; the mound stood as high as Cyan was tall. Then the bottom portion crumbled into dust and only the very top piece remained, forming a green disk. The disk slowly descended into Malaya's claw.

"This is the medal of earth," said Malaya, handing Cyan the disk. "I entrust it to you. Use it wisely."

In Cyan's hand was a green stone with a tree symbol etched into its center. It shimmered and gave off unnatural warmth as though possessing life of its own.

"You have been granted a boon, Cyan," the dragon went on, "I trust that you will use it responsibly."

"Thank you, I will," Cyan responded.

"I only hope that is the case."

Cyan showed his thanks with a bow so low that his head nearly touched the floor. It was all he could do to keep from beaming a grin over how he was that much closer to ridding himself of his curse.

"Should you ever have need of me," said Malaya, "simply call my name." There was no warmth in the dragon's words. He had spoken that last line as though it were a grudging formality.

Cyan nodded. "Thank you for putting your trust in me. But you will now excuse me, as I must be off."

"Of course," Malaya said, but his connotation was all overtones of: "Good riddance."

IX

Cyan blinked, and not a moment too soon, or the flash of green light would have blinded him. Regardless, he was bewildered to find himself in Wren's laboratory, especially since he hadn't invoked his wind charm. Wren sat at writing at his desk, not looking up to acknowledge Cyan.

"Congratulations," the wizard said flatly.

"Wren," he spat out, taken a bit by surprise.

"Yes, it is I," he said, hating to state the obvious. "I see you have the medal of earth."

Cyan looked down at the stone in his palm.

"Well, what are you waiting for?" Wren asked.

Cyan's brow furrowed. "I…"

Wren sighed and put his pen down. He glanced up from his work. "Place the medal against your bracer." Then, returning to the book on his desk, he added, "Do the same with all the others, return when you have all four."

Cyan touched the metal to his bracer. Instantly, the metal heated up from within. It was short of scalding, but still uncomfortable. The iron yielded, becoming jellylike, and accepted the medal into it.

Then it just as quickly cooled with the stone fused permanently in the armor.

"How did you know I had been given the medal?" Cyan asked.

"I could spend hours explaining magical theory to you, but I'll spare you the details. Besides, that won't help you raise your curse."

Cyan scowled. "You've taken interest in my wellbeing of late. What is it to you if I lift this curse or not?"

Wren slapped his pen down on the desktop. "I entrusted a precious magical artifact to you. Said artifact was entrusted to me. I'll need it back, or it's my job. And it's no use to me that you're too pigheaded to follow simple instructions."

"You never told me this would happen!" Cyan shouted, holding up his metal arm. "Or this!" he said, pointing to his metal leg.

"You were told all you needed to know. You're a soldier, you should be familiar with that concept."

Cyan gritted his teeth. Wren was right, and it was a point of fact he could not argue against.

"You should get going," said Wren. "The more time you spend here accomplishing nothing, the worse your affliction becomes."

"Like I don't..." Cyan yelled.

A wave of brilliant light consumed Cyan.

"…know that!" Cyan finished his sentence. It took him a moment to realize what had happened.

The claustrophobic walls of the laboratory were gone, replaced by the moss and trees that encircled the entrance of the earth shrine. Apparently, Wren was incapable of finding a good way to end a conversation, or so Cyan deduced. Or was there something that he wasn't telling him? His intuition pointed toward the latter.

His work done here, Cyan commanded the wind charm to transport him to the water shrine, and no sooner had he asked, he was falling headlong into the ocean. Cyan plunged into the water like a human missile, the force of his fall overpowering even the currents that attempted to buoy him back to the surface. His ax plummeted after him in a surge of bubbles. He yanked it out of the seabed sand and trudged into the shrine.

He walked into the inner sanctum and stopped at the center of the room. Imhra was not there, but her sea creatures were, and they swam in place eyeing him warily. Suddenly the door behind him slammed shut. He wheeled in place, then back around again and there stood Imhra, grinning.

"So," she said, "did he give you the medal or not?"

"He did," he responded, showing her the green stone on his forearm. "And it was all thanks to your help."

"It was a pleasure to lend a hand," she replied. "But now you must be true to your half of our bargain. As promised, I helped you get the earth medal, now you must fight me barehanded."

He swallowed hard. Winning a fight with a twenty-foot long dragon was nigh impossible. If that were not bad enough, she had formidable command over the element of water, as Cyan knew all too well.

"Are you ready?" she asked.

He set his weapon down. "I don't think I'll ever be as ready as I need to be to fight you."

"You're more ready now than before, now that you have Malaya's earth powers."

Cyan cocked his head to one side. "What?"

"Didn't he tell you?" Imhra could read the answer on Cyan's face. "Malaya's medal affords you power over earth, the soil, plants — you follow?"

Cyan nodded only to save face, as he really had no inkling of what she meant.

Imhra squared her shoulders in preparation for their fight.

"This isn't a fair fight," said Cyan.

"We never agreed it had to be," she said, and a horizontal column of water surged out of the wall behind her. The torrent struck Cyan dead on in the chest, toppling him onto his back. The perfectly-shaped cylinder of water pinned him flat on the ground. He clawed at the floor to inch out from under it, but it followed him, and the downpour hammered him flat. It took all his strength just to lift his head in time to see a huge gray mass rushing through the channel of water. Cyan screamed when he saw it for what it was—an enormous gray shark tore through the column of water, jaws spread wide. He kicked at the ground, flopped against the water, but to no avail.

The shark was upon him in a heartbeat. Its jaws bit down onto his torso. Cyan's breastplate gave the shark some difficulty, and while it didn't kill him immediately, the shark's jaws crushed the air out of his lungs. The pain was excruciating. He screamed, but without any air in his lungs, all that escaped him was a wheeze.

The torrent of water intensified, engulfing his face. Seawater flooded his gullet, his lungs, his stomach. His air-starved lungs burned. His chest heaved. The shark let up on its grip and adjusted, catching Cyan just beneath the ribcage. Then it reared back, tearing a gaping hole in Cyan's midsection. Blood sprang up into the torrent of water and the shark, sensing it, snapped again and again, until what was left of Cyan was the few bits splattered across the shrine floor.

* * *

Screaming his throat raw, Cyan kicked up from the ground to his feet. The shark had already begun its return trip to the perimeter wall when it heard Cyan's scream and spun in place. It paused to consider Cyan, looking bewildered inasmuch as much as sharks can look bewildered.

Imhra was ready for him. As Cyan charged her, a spring of water burst from the ground beneath him and bore him aloft. Imhra made the geyser column and the shark's torrent of water intersect, giving the shark a direct line of attack on Cyan. The shark whipped its tail into a blur as it launched itself at Cyan. Just as it smashed into him, Cyan held his arms out. The collision knocked him off the geyser spring and onto the floor on his back with the shark atop him. The shark wriggled against him, its jaws snapping inches from his face. Cyan put one hand on its snout and the other on its lower jaw, and with a mighty tug, tore the shark cleanly in two like a zipper.

Imhra gaped, horrified at the sight.

Cyan wasted no time in rushing up to her and letting fly a haymaker that caught her in the cheek. The dragon reeled with the colossal blow, toppling onto her shoulder.

The magic-induced rage waned and Cyan regained himself. Thinking quickly, he envisioned a mound of earth rising up to smother Imhra. To his surprise the ground obeyed, swelling up like a wave. Imhra quickly rolled out of the way just as the dirt crashed down. Once on her feet she leapt into the air and hovered near the shrine's ceiling, kept aloft by the repeated flapping of her wings.

"Come down here and fight!" he yelled, shaking his fist at her.

Or better yet, he thought. Cyan focused, and a column of earth sprang up beneath him, bringing him level with Imhra.

"Good thinking," she said, flitting just out of striking distance. "Only, you forgot one important fact."

Cyan got a sinking feeling.

"I can fly, and you can't," she said right before slapping the column of earth with her tail. The column sheared away into a fine spray of dirt. Cyan's back hit the water below hard. He sprang to his feet in the knee-high water, and just then it instantly froze, trapping him in place.

It grew dark in the shrine. Cyan looked up as the shadow of a giant wave overtook him, blotted out his view of the ceiling.

"That's two points for me," Imhra said from somewhere above him as the wave came rushing down. The sweep of the falling wave was perfectly aimed at his thighs, and its force sheared his torso from his fast-frozen knees. Cyan made the mistake of screaming and again his insides became heavy with seawater. The wave smashed him against the wall to his back, cracking his skull like an eggshell.

* * *

Cyan came to and scampered on all fours to the spot on the ground beneath where Imhra hovered. Once he got there he leapt up at her, arms flailing, fingers splayed to claw at her. He would never catch her—she was much too high up—at least that was what the rational part of his mind told him. That part of his mind spoke with a tinny voice from some forgotten broom closet in his head.

Laughing, Imhra descended close enough to whip her tail at him. The end of her tail hammered his chest, hurling him bodily through the air and landing him on the ground with the wind knocked out of him.

"That one's a freebie," said Imhra. "Otherwise the score would be three to nothing."

Cyan was slow in getting up. He was certain that last blow had dented his breastplate, and possibly bruised a few ribs.

"I hope you're not tired," Imhra jeered. "I can do this all day."

Just then Cyan had a flash of insight. He balled his fists and stared intently at Imhra.

"What's the matter?" she went on. "Getting frustrated?"

Cyan concentrated harder. First a patch of moss sprouted on the wall behind where Imhra hovered. The moss grew quickly, spreading across the wall. Mushrooms and flowers sprang up at the center of the growth, followed by a mass of supple vines.

The vines shot out of the wall lashed themselves around Imhra. Her wings were crushed against her body and she plummeted like a stone, landing on her face. More vines burst out of a rent in the ground and strapped her down. She struggled against them, tearing and biting at them with her jaws, but for each one she escaped four more rose up to hold her down. In the end she could barely move, her body held fast by supple green seaweed ropes.

Cyan extended an arm palm up, then squeezed his fist shut. The vines creaked as they tightened around Imhra.

"All right," she wheezed. "You score a point. Please let me go."

He clenched his fist again.

"Hey—oof!" she said. "Stop it!"

"Not unless you concede defeat," said Cyan.

She pushed her snout through to open air. "But I scored more points."

Cyan made as though to clench his fist.

"All right, all right," Imhra said. "I give up. You win."

"And that means…"

"Are you always this dense?" Imhra cut him off. She sighed. "Yes, this means you can have my medal."

Smiling, Cyan dismissed the vines. They immediately turned brown and wilted away. "My medal, please," he said, extending a hand.

Imhra shook the debris off her body. "You've had it all this time. I gave it to you before you went to see Malaya."

His jaw dropped in astonishment. "You mean this?" he said, pulling the blue stone out of his pocket and showing it to her. "I thought you gave me this just to show it to him, to convince him to give me his medal."

"I did give it to you for that same reason. He would have accepted no other proof that I trust you."

"So why couldn't I use the powers of water earlier?"

She grinned. "Because you didn't know you could." Her tone became very serious. "But now that you do know, I must warn you that you have a responsibility not to use these powers for evil. I see in

86

you a great potential for doing good, Cyan, but I also see that you might use these powers for bad ends. Please keep this in mind."

"I will," he said as he placed the medal of water against his bracer. Like the medal of earth, it fused to his armor immediately.

"Take care of yourself," she said as she crept back into the water. Once fully submerged she slowly began to fade, only her eyes remaining visible. "And if you ever need my help, just ask."

"Thank you," he said, waving goodbye to the dragon as she shut her eyes and faded completely from view.

Never one to loiter, he gripped his wind charm, instructing it to take him to the abode of the wind dragon. With two medals now in his possession, this curse would be lifted sooner than he thought, perhaps soon enough to salvage his career.

X

Cyan landed in a shallow mud hole. He rolled with the fall to make way for his ax, which he knew would be whistling down onto him in moments. Only, it didn't. Cyan stood, cupped his eyes with his hands and looked up into the sky, then scanned the landscape ahead.

"Where the hell is it?" he thought out loud.

His ax was nowhere to be seen. To make matters worse, a cold rain started to fall. He walked to the crest of a nearby hill and looked out over the land. Not far off was a farm, and he could make out the figures of people herding their animals into a barn. Thunder rumbled and the rain came down full force. Grumbling, Cyan slogged through the rain, headed for the farm.

The farm was modest at best, consisting of an old wooden granary and barn. A farmhouse sat nearby, and by the looks of it, it hadn't seen a fresh coat of paint in years. Knotholes showed through the flaking white paint. Cyan knocked on the door to the farmhouse, hoping someone would let him in before he caught pneumonia.

The door swung open. Standing in the doorframe was a spindly man in his fifties. Gray hair peeked out beneath the brim of his straw hat. He eyed Cyan up and down, then took him by the shoulder and ushered him in.

"By the gods, lad," said the farmer. "What're you doing out in the rain? You're sopping wet!"

Cyan hugged his arms to his chest, rubbed his forearms to keep warm. He sneezed.

"Take a seat," the farmer said. "I'll get you dried up in no time."

Cyan sat at the dinner table. The inside of the farmhouse, much like its outside, was also very plain. The table occupied much of what could be considered the home's foyer, and the table itself was not terribly large. An elderly lady with her hair in a tight bun emerged from the kitchen and slung a blanket over his shoulders. Cyan, shivering, wrapped it against himself for warmth.

The farmer and his wife took their seats at the table with Cyan.

"You must be crazy to be out in this weather," the farmer scolded.

Trying his best to speak with chattering teeth, Cyan asked, "Have you seen my ax?"

"If you need an ax, I'll lend you mine. Only, you're not chopping any wood today, that's for sure."

"That's not what I meant." He cut off as he felt a sneeze coming on.

The farmer's wife leaned forward, cupped Cyan's cheek in her hand. "You're cold as a corpse, son."

Cyan chortled. He knew only too well.

"We've got a spare room upstairs," said the farmer's wife. "You're welcome to it, at least until this rain passes."

She stood and took his hand, leading him to a tiny upstairs bedroom, big enough for only a bed and a short chest of drawers.

"It's not much," the farmer's wife went on, "but it's all we can offer you. Get yourself some rest. You look like you need it." With that, she backed out of the room and shut the door.

Cyan slung off his clothes and toweled himself off, hoping the metal parts of him wouldn't rust between his today's rain and his prior misadventures on the seafloor. He lay down and it felt good, so good. It had been too long since he'd slept in anything resembling a bed. Cyan shut his eyes and drifted off to sleep.

He awoke in good spirits to the smell of fresh bacon and fried potatoes. A look out his window told him he had slept straight through dinner into the following morning. He kicked off his sheets, eager to devour a plateful or more of breakfast, and planted both feet on the floor with a loud "clink!"

He froze.

"Oh no."

Cyan looked down at his legs. The curse had taken more of him—his waist down to the heels of both his feet had turned to iron. He blanched, put his hands to his mouth in shock.

The door creaked open and the farmer stepped in. Cyan's head whipped around to face him.

A note of concern darkened the farmer's face. "You look sickly, lad," he said, plodding into the room. "Stay in bed. I'll bring you your breakfast."

He returned shortly with a platter loaded with food just off the stove and still steaming. On Cyan's pewter plate were a sausage link and a slab of fried bacon atop a bed of diced skillet potatoes.

"There now," the farmer said setting the plate atop the low dresser. "While we wouldn't mind having you join us downstairs, right now you don't look in any condition to be out of bed." Then he left, shutting the door behind him.

Cyan, hungry as he was, eyed the food with disgust. The realization that there was less of him left today than yesterday had robbed him of his appetite. He picked at the food, eating without zest. He was so engrossed in worrying that he had finished his meal without noticing he was done. The only proof that he had actually eaten was his empty plate. He sighed inwardly, because while at the very least the meal had been nourishing, he would have liked to have enjoyed it. He stood and went downstairs.

Cyan turned the corner and went to the kitchen, where the farmer's wife worked cleaning the dishes. She greeted him. "Good morning."

"To you too," he muttered. He wiped his nose with his forearm. The brisk touch of metal against his nose sent a shudder down his spine. "I'm very appreciative of your hospitality, but I'm afraid I need to get going."

"No one's stopping you."

Her answer put Cyan aback. He was fully expecting her to ask for something in return for her generosity.

"Oh," he stammered. "Well, then, thanks again."

"You're welcome," she said with a smile.

"Listen, since we're already chatting, maybe I can ask you for directions. I've come looking for the wind dragon's abode..."

She smirked.

"What's so funny?" he asked.

"Everyone who comes this way asks that," she said. "The answer's always the same: I hope you brought wings."

Cyan's brow knit. "What?"

"Well whoever told you she lived in these lands played you for a fool," she went on. "She doesn't so much live in these lands as she does above them."

"You mean like on a cloud? Or on the sun?"

Cyan hoped upon a stack of deities the dragon did not live on the sun.

"She lives on a cloud," she said matter-of-factly. "Where else?"

Palms up, Cyan shrugged. Hard as it was to believe, it made perfect sense that the dragon charged with guarding the wind medal should live in the sky. After all, Cyan already knew from experience that the water dragon had made her home in the sea and the earth dragon made his in the soil. He could only wonder what the fire dragon's home would be like.

Pushing those thoughts aside, he focused his attention on the matter at hand. "Would you know where exactly she lives? Which cloud? The sky is very big, after all."

She patted his shoulder. "Don't be silly, lad. No one's been there, and no one will."

"Then how do you know she's even up there?"

"She is," she replied, pulling a soapy dish from the sink and dunking it into a bucket of clean water to rinse it off. "You've got to have faith, young man. It shows you have faith—or had—because, why would you leave home looking for her if you weren't sure she existed?"

She had him there, and Cyan nodded.

"It's been delightful chatting with you, but I must be going," said Cyan as he went for the door.

He stepped outside into a balmy, cloudless morning. Off in the distance, the farmer led his cows out to graze. He waved when he saw Cyan.

"Hello there!" the farmer called out to him.

Cyan waved back. He went to the farmer and bid him good day.

"Ah, and same to you," the farmer replied, tipping his hat.

"I really appreciate your hospitality," said Cyan.

"Oh, it's nothing at all. You'd have done the same for me, I take it."

"Certainly," Cyan lied.

"Where are you headed?"

"Well," Cyan said, and paused a beat to think. "If all I've heard is true, I'm headed straight up."

The farmer cocked his head to one side. "Oh," he said after a moment's reflection. He laughed. "Let me guess," he trailed off, pointing a finger skyward.

Cyan nodded.

"Then you'd best start flapping your wings, lad."

"Just, please, tell me where she is."

The farmer doffed his hat and scratched his head. "Well, I reckon she can't live in the sun, because if she did she'd burn up. And she can't live in the sky because she'd fall back down to the ground…"

"I get that," Cyan interrupted. "She lives on a cloud. Which one?"

The farmer chuckled under his breath.

"Which one?" Cyan pressed him.

"Son," he said, clapping his meaty hands on Cyan's shoulders. "If I didn't know any better, I'd say you were serious."

"I am."

The farmer smirked. "I don't know, lad. I never bothered to find out. Come to think of it, I don't think I ever had means of finding out."

XI

Cyan left the farmlands for the open fields he had landed in the day before. The sky dragon's shrine had to be somewhere nearby, he knew, or why would the charm drop him where it did?

Climbing to the top of the tallest hill, he cupped his eyes with his hands and scanned the heavens. Nothing stuck out as terribly unusual. Short of a handful of wispy clouds, the sky was quite empty this morning. Eventually the sunlight stung his eyes. He looked away and rubbed his eyes with his palms, cursing the farmers for believing in such ridiculous superstitions.

A cloud drifted on a swift wind and covered the sun. The day got cooler by marked degrees.

"Are you kidding me?" he said, looking up. The heavy cloud was a portent of a hard rain soon to fall.

He blinked, then again, then rubbed his eyes again because he could not believe what he saw. The passing breeze pushed the other clouds along, but not the one that blocked the sun. The big cloud clung to the sun as though anchored. Sunlight filtered through the cloud at its extremities, but not at the center. The center of the cloud cast a dark shadow onto the land below as if there were something solid there.

"I'll be damned," he said half-jokingly, then thought on how what he'd just said related all too well with his current situation, and regretted saying it.

His eyes fixed on the cloud, he paced away to where he approximated its center lay. Once he was more or less certain, he pointed a finger at the ground at his feet. Shutting his eyes, he raised that hand, palm up, in his mind envisioning himself holding a clod of dirt. The ground trembled beneath him, then rose in a solid pillar of earth. He grinned at his genius, but then got a sinking feeling when the pillar shuddered, then stopped moving altogether.

"Rise!" he yelled, thrusting his hands up. He looked over the edge. The mound had risen fifty feet, but still had plenty to go. Then it shuddered and began to sink gradually into the ground, leaving him back where he had started.

He hardly had time to gripe, for just as quickly another idea struck him.

"Wings!" he thought out loud. He shut his eyes, took a deep breath, and yelled Malaya's name at the top of his lungs. Moments later, the ground shook again as a much larger mound of dirt rose from the hillside.

Shaking the last grains of soil from his wings and back, Malaya said to him, "Ah, Cyan. I didn't think you'd need my help so soon. What do you need?"

"I need to see the wind dragon, but I have no way of getting to her shrine."

Malaya nodded. "Let me guess—you want me to fly you there?"

"If it isn't much trouble," Cyan said as unassumingly as he could. Politeness had gotten him this far, and besides, he had taken the dragon's head once and could do it again if he had to.

The dragon sighed. "Climb onto my back and I'll take you."

He lowered his neck and Cyan slung a leg over it and sat down, sliding to the base of the dragon's shoulders.

"To think," said Malaya, "at my age I'd be called on to serve as some lowly pack mule."

"You're not a pack mule, you're a steed," Cyan joshed him. "At least so long as I'm riding you."

The dragon grumbled. "All right, just hold on to my neck."

Malaya's muscles tightened as he prepared to leap up into the air. His wings opened to their fullest extent and came down in a monstrous beat, launching both him and Cyan off the ground. Malaya stayed aloft a few moments before his feet touched ground once more.

"What's the problem?" Cyan asked.

"Sorry. I haven't flown in quite a while. When you can travel in the manner that I do — rising up out of the ground anywhere in the world, I mean — flying is pointless."

Malaya crouched low to the ground and leapt into the air again, wings flailing, only to fall back on his feet once more.

Cyan dismounted and stood beside the dragon. "Some help you are."

"I'll get you where you want to go, sure enough." Malaya looked up at the cloud far above him and, without taking his eyes off of it, backpedaled step by step, then inched over to his right.

"What are you doing now?" Cyan asked.

"Calculating the distance from here to there," he answered, his eyes still skyward.

"Is it so you can gauge how very poor your flying skills are?"

Malaya shot him a glance and bared his teeth. Cyan knew better than to press his luck further.

The dragon resumed his calculations for a while longer, then turned to Cyan and said, "Stand on the X, please."

Before Cyan could ask "What X?" the grass before his feet dried up and shriveled, leaving a brown dirt square containing an area of healthy grass in the shape of an X. Cyan did as the dragon said and asked, "Now what?"

Malaya responded with a question. "You do know how a lever works, don't you?"

"What does that have to do with anything?"

"Everything." Malaya bent low to the ground, looking like he was about to take another attempt at flying. "Now you go to see the sky dragon." He leapt into the air and hit the ground on all fours, sending a tremor across the hillside. The ground upon which he landed sank as the soil beneath Cyan's feet pitched up suddenly, catapulting Cyan skyward, sending him whizzing up like an arrow though the air.

Cyan coasted to the peak of his arc, bringing his chest level to the cloud. Malaya had fallen short of his mark by a few inches. Cyan clawed at the open air, clenching his fingers around the shrine's stone front stoop. He dangled there, legs flailing, his body except for his hands immersed in the cloud, regretting not having done daily calisthenics since his promotion to captain.

His fingers supported the whole weight of his body but the pain was all in his arms. He could almost feel the corded muscles in his forearms shredding apart. He raised his head and rested his chin on the shrine's doorstep. Then he slung an arm over the edge and latched onto an upraised tile in the floor, and using this as a handhold he pulled a leg up as well. The tile gave way and he slid down to where he started, hanging by both arms, as the yellow tile fell to the earth below. He watched as it plunged and became too small to see long before hitting the ground.

The air soon grew thick with humidity. Water beaded on his forehead. It occurred to him that rain clouds had blown in and merged with this cloud. The surface he clung to grew slippery. Thunder blasted in the distance, resounding loudly in his ears. The wind kicked up. Another peal of thunder rang out, this time closer than before. Desperately he clawed at the ledge, knowing he had to get out of the cloud before the storm got any worse. His fingers dug into the grout between the floor tiles, searching for a handhold to safety.

A white flash tore the sky apart that moment. The thunderclap that followed made his ears ring. His head lolled on his shoulders. The world spun.

He let go.

There was another flash as the sky lit up and paid glorious homage to the man who was Cyan Wraithwate, and then there was nothing.

* * *

Cyan awoke, his body still sizzling from the blast of lightning that had just killed him. He came around abruptly as always, and screaming a war cry that rivaled the thunder above. The word kill was stamped indelibly in his mind with white-hot brands, as it was all he could think about. He was so engrossed that it never occurred to him how quickly the ground drew nearer. And he never once gave it any thought how his body would be strewn out for yards in every direction on hitting the ground, which is exactly what happened.

* * *

Cyan's eyes tore open and he found himself facedown in the grass. He leapt to his feet, in the center a man-sized depression a few inches in depth. His arms trembled, his fingers hooked into angry white-knuckle claws. He sat on his haunches, gnashing his teeth and shuddering with frustration.

There was nothing around to kill. All around were rolling hills of healthy green grass. Frustrated to the point of foaming at the mouth, Cyan clenched his fists, digging his fingers into his palms. His metal gauntlets yielded slightly under the pressure. That was when it occurred to his primeval mind that grass was a living thing.

He dropped to his knees and tore at the grass with both hands, ripping the blades into pieces and flinging them over his shoulder. Face to the ground he tore at the grass with his teeth, spitting out mouthful after mouthful.

Once through with grazing, he stood up and stamped his heels into the ground, turning up the soil, then began to tear the grass from the earth in strips. By the time he was through, the hill he had landed on was almost completely bald except for a few patches he had missed.

The rage finally worked out of him, he slumped forward, his palms resting on his knees, and caught his breath. He looked up at the cloud from which he had fallen. It hovered in place as the storm clouds that had caused him to die twice consecutively slowly drifted on. Soon the heavens were for the most part clear, with the occasional white cloud floating in the blue plane of sky.

Seeing that Malaya had already returned to the earth, he decided to try his luck with the water dragon. Moments after calling her name, a heavy mist began to form from thin air before him. The vapor took the shape of a dragon and gradually became opaque until at last it dissipated, blown away by the wind, and where the dragon-shaped mist had been stood Imhra.

"Hey Cyan," she said. "Need anything?"

"I do. Would you please take me to the wind dragon's shrine?"

She looked up at the cloud hovering above their heads. "Sure, I'll fly you there."

Cyan cast her a skeptical glance.

"What's wrong?" she asked. "Are you afraid of heights?"

"No." Then he thought his answer over some, considering the recent past. "Yes."

"Climb on." She lowered her head and he climbed onto her back in the same manner as he had done with Malaya. "Hold tight," she said, just before leaping up into the air and flapping her wings to gain altitude.

The ground below shrank quickly as they flew upward in a wide spiral. Before long she set foot on the shrine's stone doorstep, and she promptly let him off.

"Be careful not to fall," she cautioned him.

A shudder ran through him.

"What's the matter?" she asked, noticing that he had become uneasy.

"Nothing," he spat out.

She shrugged. "If you want help getting down, don't hesitate to call me again," she added before disappearing into mist.

XII

Cyan turned and faced the shrine. It looked similar to the others he had seen on his journey— round, tall, and presumably made of stone. An intricate pattern of small yellow tiles lined the narrow pathway to the front door of the shrine. He paced slowly toward the door, being careful to stay in the approximate center of the path for fear of losing his balance or being blown over the edge by a strong wind. The doors to the shrine were shut but unlocked, and he carefully pulled them open and stepped inside.

The interior was dark, except for where the sunlight cast vibrant colors through the stained glass windows. Yellow tiles of all shades covered the walls and the floor, arranged in chevron patterns leading to the shrine's heart. Above the doors to the inner sanctum was a horizontal ledge upon which sat an intricately carved and painted statue of a half-bird, half-man hybrid. The statue stooped on the ledge like a gargoyle, its head held low to glower at intruders. A three-pronged lance was in its grip.

Cyan stopped in place, startled by the statue. He approached it warily, waved a hand before its eyes to make certain it was not alive.

He cupped his mouth. "Hey!" he yelled into the statue's face. It did not move.

Cyan pressed on to the door leading to the inner sanctum. No sooner had he set a hand on the door's brass ring than a voice called out from behind him.

"Stop!"

Cyan wheeled around and watched as a birdman, identical to the statue sitting above his head, flew from a ledge above the shrine entrance. Perched there, Cyan had walked directly beneath it and failed to notice it even was there.

The birdman landed a short distance before him. Its majestic falcon head darted to and fro, eyes locked on Cyan. He paced forward on yellow clawed feet, keeping the end of his trident level to the warrior's chest.

"I am Basp," the birdman said. "I guard this shrine. What business have you here?"

"I seek an audience with the wind dragon."

"What do you want with her?"

"The medal she protects."

Basp screeched. "You'll not have it! I sense you are an evil man, you are unworthy!"

Cyan reached behind his back and just then remembered he did not have his ax. He swallowed hard. Without his weapon, the birdman and his eight-foot-long lance would make swift work of him. Cyan backed away until he was up against the door.

"Die!" Basp thrust his lance, puncturing Cyan's armor and running him through with all three blades. Just as he felt his body slacken, the birdman pulled a latch mounted on the grip of his weapon. A spring mechanism built into the lance discharged with a loud snap. The two outer tines of Basp's trident flew out and away from each other in a wide arc before collapsing into the shaft. Cyan's upper torso was snipped cleanly from his body and fell alongside his legs, spurting blood everywhere.

* * *

Cyan sprang to his feet, much to the surprise of Basp. Fists clenched in hate, muscles corded tight to the point of snapping, he charged the off-guard birdman on all fours, pawing the ground with his hands like an animal. With an alarmed squawk Basp leapt into the air and beat his wings, getting him safely out of reach. Cyan jumped up at him from below, intent on catching hold of the Basp's feet and beating him to a bloody pulp.

"Evil sustains you, demon!" said Basp, hovering in place. "Why else would you not die after I vanquished you?"

A white froth bubbled from Cyan's mouth. He had the look of a rabid dog.

"I put you down once, and I can do it again!" the birdman jeered. He squinted, locked in deep concentration.

A strong wind spun at Cyan's heels, growing ever stronger. The whirlwind swept Cyan off his feet and into Basp's downpointed trident, impaling him. He sputtered as blood welled up between his lips. With his last bit of strength he made a drunken swipe at Basp. The birdman dropped his weapon and Cyan fell with it, hitting the ground with a wet splatter.

* * *

Cyan awoke, screaming and thrashing like a man possessed.

"Hold still," Basp ordered, dragging Cyan by his ankles. "You're not making this any easier."

They were outside, near the precipice. Despite the blind rage burning within him, the warrior realized what was going on. The birdman intended to hurl his body to the ground below—Cyan could not let that happen.

He shook a leg free and kicked Basp in the ankle, causing him to double over and clutch at his injured foot. He then reared up and shoved the hunched-over birdman over the edge with both feet and made a sprint for the shrine. He had not gone halfway when Basp swooped in from above and shoved his trident point-down into Cyan's path.

"You forgot that I have wings," the birdman said. "Heed me, it is I who shall be rid of you."

Basp jabbed with his weapon and Cyan skipped back in time for the blades to slice nothing but open air. As Basp drew back for another stab, Cyan rushed in, shoving past Basp as he made a run for the shrine's inner chamber.

Basp wheeled in place and shouted after him. "There's nowhere for you to hide." He stood in the doorway, his trident trained to run Cyan through as he advanced into the shrine.

Cyan took a breath to settle himself and concentrated, forming a mental image of a wave at sea. His body was soon engulfed in mist.

"What trickery is this?" said Basp. "You, a mage?" He squawked a laugh. "I think not!" He flapped his wings and took to the air.

"I'll show you," said Cyan, thrusting out both arms. The mist condensed into a powerful stream of water that shot at Basp, striking with enough force to knock him out of the air. He recovered in mid-fall and righted himself in time to get blasted by another surge of water. This time, the surge smashed him against the shrine's wall. He crumpled against it and slid down, collapsing to the shrine's floor on his face.

Basp stood and shook his head. "You are not quite as dimwitted as I thought, if you are disciplined enough to command some form of magic." He paused and rubbed the hurt out of the sides of his beak.

"Let me through," said Cyan as he readied another volley.

"Never!"

Cyan fired and missed. The birdman retook his perch over the doorway and raised his trident. His feathers puffed up.

Cyan launched a jet of water more powerful than the first. At that instant Basp let fly a white bolt of lightning that carried through the stream of water and struck Cyan in the chest. The shrine's windows blew apart and shattered the moment the bolt made contact with him, and Cyan's reaction to the blast of raw energy was not much different.

* * *

Cyan sprang erect with eyes bloodshot and hands trembling to wring Basp's neck. The birdman crouched on his roost, panting from exhaustion.

"You..." he began, bracing himself against his weapon. "You live. I did not think you would come back after I gave it my all just now. And yet you still live."

Cyan gnashed his teeth in response.

"Regardless of how many times I kill you," Basp went on, "know that I will continue to do so until you stop returning or I fall dead."

Cyan ran at full speed at the birdman, who leapt up into the air and out of reach. With both hands Basp raised his trident and plunged it down, aiming for the top of Cyan's skull, but the warrior quickly sidestepped the blow and latched on to the shaft of the birdman's weapon. He gave the trident a sharp tug, yanking Basp out of the air. Basp hit the ground and a mess of feathers burst in every direction upon impact.

Trident still in hand, Cyan placed the tines of the weapon at the base of his adversary's neck, wanting so very badly just to lean forward and sink the blades into his feathered flesh. His arms trembled expectantly.

"Go on, finish me," Basp taunted.

"Shut up!" Cyan shouted. The mere sound of Basp's voice goaded him to kill the birdman. It took all he had not to run him through.

"Don't you want to see my mistress? She will see you die, I promise you."

Cyan booted him in the head with the tip of his foot, not too hard, but hard enough to show that he meant business. "I have defeated you, now show me to the wind dragon," he said through clenched teeth.

"I am not beaten until you kill me. And even then, I have won."

Part of him seriously wanted—needed—to kill the birdman, and whether that desire sprang from him or his magic-induced rage, Cyan was unable to tell. He pressed the blades against the birdman's neck until he drew blood. The tines were murderously sharp.

"Stop being so difficult!" he yelled.

"What if I won't, what will you do? Kill me?" Basp laughed. "I fear not death."

He threw down the spear. Crouching, Cyan grabbed the top of Basp's head and pulled him close so he could scream in his face.

"Don't you see I don't want to kill you?" Cyan yelled. "I didn't want to fight you in the first place!"

Basp's beady eyes looked on icily.

"Look," Cyan said in lowered tones. "I'll agree to let bygones be bygones if you would please let me have an audience with the wind dragon." He let go of Basp and stood.

The birdman was slow in rising to his feet. "I still don't trust you," he said with arms crossed. "But if you want to speak to my mistress so badly, then you might as well." Under his breath he added, "Maybe she can kill you for good."

Basp pulled open the chamber door and motioned for Cyan to enter.

XIII

Cyan was beginning to think that the same architect of the first two shrines designed them all. This shrine's heart looked almost identical to the others he had seen. The room was perfectly round and its walls extended very high up, but unlike the others, its ceiling was not fully enclosed. Looking up from the bottom hinted at what it might be like to look up from the depths of a dry well. Below his feet was a huge mosaic of three white lines against a yellow background, a representation of wind blowing across the land. And as was the case in his previous encounters with the dragons, the wind dragon was not readily visible.

"Anyone home?" he called out. His words echoed within the chamber momentarily then faded into silence. "Wind dragon, are you here?"

No reply came.

He stepped away from the entrance and stood at the center of the chamber. A breeze swept in from above, circling around the room. Gradually it increased in strength and began to swirl around him. What followed he did not expect—the wind plucked him off his feet and flung him skyward, out the top of the shrine, slowing down only to let him off softly on the roof.

Cyan stood, inadvertently casting his gaze over the edge. The view from up here was staggering—he could see for miles across the countryside. Vertigo made his knees quiver. He tottered back from the edge.

"Why have you come?" asked a voice from behind him.

Cyan, caught off guard, jumped up in surprise and nearly lost his balance.

"Be careful now," it went on. "It's quite a drop from up here."

He already knew it was.

Cyan turned around and his eyes came across the yellow-scaled wind dragon lying on her back, apparently sunning herself. Her head rested upon her fore-claws; her eyes were shut as she soaked in the sun's warmth.

"Wind dragon," he began as he approached, "I need to discuss something important with you."

"I'll say," she responded, her eyes still shut. "I can't imagine the trouble you must have gone through just to come and see me up here." She looked at him. "That, and getting by Basp." She rolled her eyes, then shut them again. "I heard it all the way up here."

"I'm sorry about the windows."

"You really must have something important to say, after having gone through all this."

"Wind dragon..."

"Stop with that. You needn't call me wind dragon," she said with fax gravity. "Call me by my name, Fandi. And you are Cyan Wraithwate."

"Yes," he said, put off. "How did you..."

"Your reputation precedes you," she said.

Something about the way she spoke made it apparent that she knew of him. Although her manner gave no outward clues — she lay there with eyes shut, calm as ever — there was something about her way of saying his name just then. It made him uneasy.

"If you say so," he said. "I've come for..."

"No."

"I've not even said..."

"Your past runs faster than you ever will travel."

"Stop interrupting me!"

She raised an eyelid and shot an angry one-eyed glare at Cyan. For an instant Cyan's heart felt as though it had stopped beating.

"Then, what can I do for you?" she asked.

Cyan cleared his throat. "I've come to ask you for... would you please stop that?"

She paused, her mouth open partway. She had silently mouthed each of his words as he had said them. "You're wasting your time, Cyan. I know every single unflattering detail of your life."

Cyan blanched.

"And knowing this," she went on, "coupled with the fact that you barge in here and ruin my day, only makes me less inclined to speak to you any longer. Show yourself out, if you please. Over the side of the cloud is the fastest way."

A lump caught in Cyan's throat. "I… I'm sorry."

"No, you're not."

"Really, I am sorry. I'm just… I'm just not very good at apologies." He looked down at his feet. "I'm sorry."

She watched him keenly. "That one actually sounded genuine."

"I've been practicing," he said, shrugging his shoulders.

"What is on your mind, Cyan?"

"I thought you knew."

"Humor me," she said flatly. "I don't get much opportunity for conversation up here."

A question stuck out in his mind just then that he had to know the answer to. "Then why do you need a shrine guardian if no one can reach you?"

"One can't be too careful."

Cyan knit his fingers. "I suppose I should start with why I'm here." He sighed. "I am cursed. This armor I wear was fashioned by devils. With every passing day, it steals more of me and leaves behind lifeless metal. And I can't take it off unless I gather the medals of the elements."

He raised his forearm and showed her the two disks embedded in the bracer. "Right now I have two of the medals. I have come asking you to lend me yours."

Her eyes widened at this. Cyan could not tell whether she did this solely to further their conversation, or whether she was genuinely surprised that her colleagues would lend him their support.

"They did test you first, right?" she asked.

"Yes."

"Then I suppose I must test you also."

Cyan bit his tongue for not lying to her when he had the chance.

She held a talon to her mouth and chewed at it. Although he had never seen a dragon do this, it seemed to him as though she was doing some serious thinking.

"You must understand," she said, "I don't do this very often. Honestly, you've caught me off guard. I don't have any tests in mind for you."

His heart leapt—he might actually get the wind medal without first undergoing a test. "So you'll let me…"

"I just thought of something," she cut him off.

An infant's cradle appeared to her immediate left, and within it was a human baby no older than six months. This was no ordinary infant—its flesh shone like gold. The baby gurgled and cooed happily in its soft bed as Cyan leaned over to glimpse at it.

"I want you to throw this baby over the edge," said Fandi.

He balked at her request. "What?"

"This is the indestructible golden baby," the wind dragon said. "It is immortal. I want you to pitch it over the edge."

The warrior glanced at Fandi, then at the cradle, then back at Fandi, all with an eyebrow raised. He could not believe what he'd just heard.

"You are sure you want me to do this?" he asked.

She nodded.

Not hesitating a moment, he grabbed the cradle with both hands and heaved it over his head, hurling it downward with a mighty toss. Down the infant plunged, cradle and all as in the nursery rhyme, as both Cyan and Fandi watched from above. Moments later the cradle smashed into the ground and left a tiny crater where it splintered into pieces.

"Wow, you sure are heartless," Fandi said, turning to face Cyan.

"You said he was indestructible."

Her eyes grew wide. "You just threw a human baby from a cloud."

"It's not human if it's immortal," he said, thinking quickly.

"Then clearly neither are you."

Her words stung Cyan to the marrow of his bones.

Suddenly the cradle with its occupant appeared beside them, where it had been before he had thrown it down. Cyan leaned over the side of the cradle and took another look at the infant — it was not injured in the least. The baby's golden skin showed no evidence of even a bruise.

"You're a meanie," the baby said quite clearly before vanishing instantly, taking his cradle with him.

"You're lucky there are no such things as golden babies, Cyan," she chastised him. "Because if there were, you would have killed this one." She paused. "I am afraid that you have failed your test."

"No," he spat out. "No! I only did what you told me to do!"

"Don't you know evil when you see it? Because I do, and you are an evil man."

"Test me again — please!" he begged her. "I'll get it right this time!"

"That would not prove anything."

"Is it not enough that two other elemental dragons trust me?"

"It was enough to convince me to test you."

"But..." He was running out of ideas. "If you don't lend me your medal, then you will be the one who damns me to an eternity in iron."

"You did that to yourself." She sighed, knowing what she would say next she simply had to say, even though she knew it could be cause for remorse later. "I am sympathetic, but I cannot lend you my medal. You have my apologies."

"But," he stammered. "Don't you see in me a great potential to repent and turn away from my past life of evil?"

"You've been speaking with Imhra haven't you?" she asked. "Well, to answer your question, yes and no. Yes, because you might be a man of your word. No, because you might just be a charismatic liar bent on keeping the powers of the elements for yourself. Right now, my convictions are leaning toward the latter."

A chessboard popped into existence between them.

"Do you play, Cyan?" she asked.

"What does..."

"Since you're not lifting your curse anytime soon and you're doomed for all eternity, you and I may as well get some games in."

Cyan rubbed his chin. "If I win, you must lend me your medal of wind."

"No."

He winced inwardly.

"And it's not like you're going to win, either," she said. "I haven't lost a game in twelve hundred years. Now, if you lose, what do I get?" She cut him off before he could answer. "Wait, I know—if I win, I take your soul."

He swallowed hard. "That's hardly fair."

"Such is life, Cyan. You didn't ask to be cursed, just as I didn't ask that you storm into my shrine and cause such a ruckus." She advanced a white pawn. "Your move, Cyan."

A fine sweat broke on Cyan's brow. Hesitantly, he reached for a black knight and made his move.

Their game lasted hours. Cyan plotted out every move, often taking several minutes before reaching for his pieces. This was no leisurely game and he had too much at stake to be careless. In contrast Fandi breezed through her turns, snapping up her pieces just as quickly as Cyan had set his down. It annoyed him to no end that she played so fast and easy, especially since he had so much riding on the outcome of this game, and she had nothing to lose.

It was evening by the time their game ended in stalemate. He fumed inside not because he was beaten—because he wasn't—but because he had lost so much time and not won.

"Good game," she admitted. "You didn't win, but if it's any consolation that's the closest I've come to losing to a mortal."

"May I please have the medal of wind?"

She glowered at him. "Is that all you think about? You're lucky I didn't just take your soul."

Cyan put up his hands in a conciliatory gesture.

"But," she went on, her eyes locked on his. "There's nothing stopping me from doing that right now."

Cyan's knees slackened. She never broke her stern glare. He could almost feel his soul being ripped from him and drawn toward the dragon.

She smiled, and it was a sight when she did, because her lips pulled back to reveal a full mouth of serrated teeth.

"Calm down, would you?" she said, laughing. "I had no intention of ever taking your soul."

He breathed a quiet sigh of relief.

"I doubt you even had one," she added.

He gave a strained chuckle.

"Listen," she went on. "Our game has given me time to think. You might just merit a second chance."

Cyan grinned ear to ear.

"But only one," she intoned, holding up a talon to make her point. "There is no such thing as a second second chance, so you'd better make this count."

He nodded that he understood.

"And that is if I decide to grant you one," she said. "See me again in a few days after I have thought this over some more. I will grant you a wind charm so that you can return here easily."

"I already have one," he spoke up, showing her his charm.

Her eyes widened. "How did you get that? I don't give them out to just anybody."

"A mage by the name of Wren gave me this one."

She thought silently for a moment. "I don't know anyone by that name."

"You mean to say you know everything about me and yet nothing about this mage?"

She snarled at him. "My powers are vast, but not infinite."

"Okay, okay," he replied, putting up his hands once more. "Perhaps he manufactured his own wind charm?"

"Likely." She paused a beat. "I would be careful around him. Wind charms are not easy to make. If he made one himself, it speaks of his abilities."

Cyan sneered. "Why should I be afraid of some half-pint mage?" He crossed his arms. "You should have seen the thrashing I gave him earlier. I got him by the collar and…"

The serious look on Fandi's face made him stop midsentence.

"Someone that powerful might have a greater agenda," she said. "If you say he is helping you, then it may be because you further his interests somehow."

"He did say his superiors would chastise him if he didn't return the bracer."

"And he promised to help you obtain the four medals of the elements, so you could take it off?"

He nodded.

"No doubt by now you've seen how powerful the medals are?" she said. "Say you gather them all and he helps you lift your curse. Then what?"

"Then..." he trailed off. Cyan rubbed his chin. He hadn't thought that far ahead.

"Do you suppose," Fandi went on, "he might just take the medals for himself?"

"I wouldn't put it past him."

She nodded. "This mage, Wren, may not have your best interests in mind. Be wary of whose interests your efforts serve."

Cyan gave a firm nod. He understood her more even than she may have intended. Cyan only ever served his own interests, even at the expense of others, and would work to further others' aims only if he would benefit from it. His methods had gotten him so far as captaincy of his unit and hadn't failed him yet.

"Let me make you a new wind charm," Fandi said.

"No need. I mean, no thank you," he corrected himself.

"Are you sure?" she asked, as though he was the first ever to have turned down the offer of a genuine wind charm. "As you wish. Ah, wait just a second."

She plodded over to the other side of the shrine's roof, returning with an ax in her claws.

"This struck the roof of my home the other day," she said. "It came close to taking my head off."

Cyan smirked.

"If you know who it belongs to, please return it to its owner," she went on.

"It's mine actually," he said with a sheepish grin. "Sorry."

"However did it end up here?"

"The wind charm. I invoked it to bring me here, but instead it dropped me in the middle of a field. I guess my ax got to where I wanted to go."

She shook her head. "That's shoddy craftsmanship."

"It suits my purposes well enough," he said, gripping it in his fist. "I will see you soon."

He invoked the charm, commanding it to take him to the abode of the fire dragon. The green wind swirled around him, lifting him off his feet.

Everything disappeared in a bright flash and before he could open his eyes he knew he was on his way.

XIV

The feeling of the wind whipping past his body told that he was — as always — falling facedown out of the sky toward his destination. He braced for impact, bringing his hands up to cover his face. The wind charm had already broken his nose once, and he'd be a fool if he'd let that happen to him again.

Cyan's fall lasted markedly longer this time. He opened his eyes and hardly had time to scream as he plummeted face first in a direct path toward the abode of the fire dragon — the bubbling crater of an active volcano. He hit the surface of the glowing magma with a "plop!" and was incinerated at once.

* * *

Cyan leapt out of the jellied magma like a flying fish, a spray of liquid flame trailing his path through the air. His body charred to powder as quickly as it had been made whole again by the bracer's magic. He belly-flopped onto the surface of the molten rock and it bore his smoldering body up. The pain was excruciating for an instant — then his nerves seared away and left nothing but a persistent, icy tingling. With his last ounce of strength, he flung an arm ahead of him and clawed his way across the field of magma, his body fraying away all the while. His fingers charred away to a stump, then his forearm and arm, and he collapsed bodily into the inferno.

* * *

He snapped to and kicked to the surface, launching him out of the volcano crater like an arrow shot from the tallest longbow. His body whistled through the air, still alight and smoldering in patches as he shot upward. He reached the apex of his climb and windmilled down in a clumsy arc. He sank into the liquid flames with a muffled splash and burst out once more with parts of him seared off. If dolphins could swim in flames, they would look very much like he did now.

On his third bounce he landed on his shoulder, and it too was eaten away. With too much of him gone, he thrashed and made a feeble hop before sinking back into the gulf of glowing fire.

* * *

The skin had hardly knit over Cyan's flaming bones when he burst from the crater in an arc of fire, shrieking from the bottom of a throat that hadn't fully regained its shape. He soared over the edge of the crater and pitched over its side. The ground was all flat stones, like roof shingles, but sharp and scaldingly hot. Cyan tumbled over and over down the steep mountainside, scraping himself everywhere and searing his exposed skin.

He rolled over onto his back, panting from the unbearable heat below. Even the rocks let up steam that caused his vision to ripple. He coughed, and when he did it was weak. Each breath sucked down dry, heavy air that parched his lungs and left him feeling faint.

Sweat poured from his forehead. His hair clung to his face in matted heaps. He thought to brush the hair from his eyes and found that he could not move. His brain ached; he could feel it broiling within his skull.

His chest heaved. He was suffocating. He opened his mouth to its fullest, looking like a fish on dry land, and struggled to draw breath. His tongue folded onto itself and stuck to the insides of his dry mouth. He lacked the strength to move even his tongue. Everything went gray. The haze of black that had ringed his field of vision marched in on the center. Overcome at last, his eyes rolled back in their sockets as he lost consciousness.

* * *

He awoke with a gasp and his eyes opened onto nothing but black. He squeezed his eyelids shut and strained to open them, but could still see nothing. It took a few moments to register that his eyes were, in fact, open, and he was blind.

The realization froze him to the core — the cursed armor had finally taken his face. He gritted his teeth and thrashed, but found he could not move.

"No!" he yelled, straining to flail his limbs. "No!"

It had finally happened. The armor had taken him completely. He could not move, or see, or feel. He was doomed to spend eternity trapped within the confines of a body that was his in name alone, and now was nothing more than a lifeless husk of metal.

"No!" he screamed, but it was all wasted effort, as there was no one to hear him. He broke down into sobs.

"Quiet."

Cyan jerked at the sound of someone else's voice. Had it sounded feminine? He wasn't sure from how abruptly it had come on. He groaned inwardly.

Almost as bad as being trapped forever in his own mind was having to share it with another person. Worse—a girl. He held his breath and turned his head, searching out its source.

A brusque hand grabbed him by the mouth and pulled his jaws open. Something cold ran down his face. Water flowed into his mouth and he coughed it out; some had run into his lungs.

The water stopped abruptly.

"Stop that. Now drink."

What felt like the rim of an earthenware jug was pressed to his lips. It tipped forward, spilling water onto his face. Water, crisp and pure, ran down into his throat to his stomach; he could feel it cooling all the way down. He drank until he was out of breath.

"Where am I?" he asked.

"Safe," said the voice.

"Where?" he demanded.

"Tell me how you feel."

The question caught him off guard. "Fair."

The person with him sighed. "You were almost dead when we found you. You're lucky to be alive."

He snickered. "You don't know the half of... wait..."

It dawned on him that he must not have been turned fully into iron.

"Hey," he called out, wriggling his arms. They wouldn't budge, but as his senses returned he realized that he was bound down to a sort of cot. He lay on his back, unable to move.

"Where am I? And why am I tied up?" he asked in a panic. "Answer me!"

Her response was slow in coming. "You are safe."

"I know that!"

"That is all I am allowed to tell you right now," she said apologetically.

All of a sudden a sheet of heavy black fabric was raised from his eyes. He could see, although just barely. Everything was a blur, and wherever he was, it was dark as a cave. Tiny fires at sparse intervals lit up the room.

His companion knelt over him. He could see her only in outline.

"I can't see," Cyan said.

"The fire has damaged your sight. It will come back with time, but all you can do about that now is rest."

She put her hand to his forehead and he winced as searing pain ignited in his face.

"Your skin is still very red from being too close to the fire," she said. All went black once more as she placed a wet sheet of fabric over his eyes. The fabric was itchy and tough, almost like tree bark, but the water it had soaked up soothed his aching skin.

He then felt a finger on his lower lip pushing downward to open his mouth.

"You must eat now," she told him.

"I'm not..." he said, but cut off as bland mush fell into his mouth. He chewed at it disinterestedly and swallowed, and opened his mouth for another helping.

"It doesn't taste very good, I know," she said, "but you'll be fed better once your health improves."

"Please," he said between mouthful. "You have to tell me where I am."

Then was silence, and then she sighed out her nostrils. "You are beneath Mount Kierns."

"Where?"

"Shh!" She held a hand to his mouth to keep him quiet.

"Do you mean we're in a mine?" he whispered.

"I don't know. I don't know what a mine is."

Cyan shook his head. "Describe where we are to me."

She thought a moment. Wherever she was from, it must have been difficult to describe it to someone not from there, or so Cyan deduced from how long it took her to answer.

"You are within the mountain where we found you. We live in the mountain, away from the lava."

His eyebrows shot up his forehead. "Is this the lair of the fire dragon?"

"What do you mean by dragon?"

"You know, big scary lizard, plods around on four legs, lots of teeth, scales, a tail…"

She gasped quietly. "You'll not talk about him like that. You're such a fool to have come here, if seeing him was your aim. Our home is dangerous for your type."

"What… what do you mean by that?"

A muffled commotion from a short distance away snagged his attention.

"I have to go now," she said.

"But…"

"No," she stopped him short. "Sleep for now. It will do you good."

She got up from his bedside before he could protest any further. Her footsteps grew softer as she paced away in a hurry.

XV

However long he had lain on the cot Cyan had no way of knowing. The furthest thing on his mind was sleep, and indeed, he was incapable of it because his mind was so preoccupied. All the while he worried he might miss his appointment with Fandi back at the wind shrine, or that she had changed her mind about giving him a second chance, to say nothing of how much he worried he might spend the rest of his life a bound-up prisoner of the people who lived under the mountain.

His ears perked to footfalls drawing nearer.

"Who's there?" he called out.

"It is I," said the familiar voice. She sat down beside him.

"I don't even know your name."

"Terlu," she said it slowly, as though it would give him difficulty repeating it.

"My name is Cyan."

She touched his face. "Your skin is not as hot as before. That is good."

"What time is it?"

"The moon is at three quarters of the way down the sky. Soon it will be day."

"What day is it?"

"I told you, it is night."

Terlu could not have seen it, as Cyan had a moist rag over his face, but he rolled his eyes at having to simplify what he thought should be obvious.

"What day of the week is it?" he asked.

"Explain what a week is."

An exasperated little breath huffed out of Cyan's mouth. "You don't know what a week is?"

Terlu hesitated to answer. By her silence, Cyan surmised that Terlu or her people had no notion of time.

"Never mind that," he said.

Terlu pressed the lip of the water jug against his mouth.

"Drink," she said as she tipped it forward. Cyan had a hard time putting it all down without drowning. He gasped for breath when it was empty.

"You need to be more gentle with that thing," he said.

She chuckled. "I see your strength is returning. That is good."

He smiled out of politeness alone. "Terlu, I do appreciate your helping me, but I have to be going soon. So, if you please, would you untie me?"

"Where are you going?"

He moistened his lips with a flick of his tongue. "I know nothing of Mount Kierns. I'm just a traveler."

"You said that. Tell me where you are headed."

He clenched his jaw. Faced with no other alternative, he decided on telling her the truth. "I've come looking for the fire dragon."

"Father Hasaq," she corrected him. "You must have tried to go directly to him, then."

"Why am I all bound up?"

There was tense silence for a long string of moments.

"Why am I tied up?" Cyan asked, more firmly this time.

"Because..." she cut off. "Because we think you are a monster."

Cyan's jaw dropped. "What? How?"

"We—I—saw you fall into the volcano crater. You leapt out and fell back in again many times, and yet you live. You swam in the fire like Father Hasaq. No one ever has done such a thing. You are either a monster or a god."

"Or both," Cyan muttered under his breath. "Terlu, which do you think I am?"

"We," she said with emphasis, "think you are a monster, but it is up to Father Hasaq to decide."

"Very well, then take me to him."

"In due time, Cyan."

Her hands grazed the sides of his head, removed the moist fabric from his eyes.

His vision gradually came into focus. Cyan was in some sort of subterranean cave. Brass sconces hung from the bare earth walls, but the tiny room was still uncomfortably dim.

An enormous red-scaled lizard leaned over him. She sat with her legs folded beneath her and her hands in her lap. She watched Cyan with her pair of solid black eyes, eyes that looked more at home on the face of a child's doll than on a living thing.

He jerked in surprise. "I thought you…"

"You thought I was human like you?" she cut him off. "Would it have made any difference?"

Cyan blinked, then again, staring dumbly at her as he tried to make sense of his predicament.

"Are you the dragon of fire?" he asked.

"I am not Father Hasaq. I am Terlu."

Cyan nodded that he understood. Still, it was a question worth asking. Two more lizards entered from the hall behind them and stood flanking the doorway. Each had a spear in his fist.

"Is he well?" asked one.

"His vision has returned," Terlu responded.

The lizard who had spoken stepped forward and eyed Cyan over. His dark ruddy scales sagged a little and looked almost brown in the dim light. He was markedly taller than his companion. Of the three lizards in the room, this one looked the eldest.

The old lizard drew a step closer, then prodded Cyan in the ribs with the butt of his spear.

"Hey!" said Cyan.

"The man speaks," said the lizard, sounding as surprised as amused. "Terlu rescued you from the fire pit. She owns you now."

Cyan glowered. "No one owns me." He cut short when the lizards leveled their spears at Cyan's face. "What are you going to do?" he went on. "Your weapons cannot hurt me."

He watched for a reaction. The lizard with whom he had spoken remained steady, but his younger companion was markedly shaken. The young one's spear trembled in his grip.

"You saw what I can do," Cyan said. "I swam in the fire like Father Hasaq."

"Blasphemy!" said the old lizard, and cocked his arm for a thrust.

"Terlu saw!" Cyan shot back.

The old lizard froze in place. Terlu's eyes grew wide and the old lizard caught her expression. She looked away.

"And he did too," Cyan lied, indicating the other lizard with his eyes.

"Me?" the young lizard stammered. "I…"

"Is this true?" asked the old lizard. His eyes darted between Terlu and the young male.

"I know you're afraid of me," Cyan pressed them. "That's why I'm tied up. And I know why you're afraid of me, too." He lowered his tone to a growl. "Take me to see Father Hasaq, now."

"And if we do not?" said the old one.

Cyan glowered at him. As he hadn't yet thought of what to say, silence and a hard look served him well enough.

The tension broke on the old lizard's face. "Terlu, Ranthe, pick up the cot and take him to Father Hasaq."

The two younger lizards arranged themselves one at the foot of Cyan's cot, the other at its head. Between the two of them they easily hefted the cot off the ground and marched out the door with it.

They left the burrow Cyan had found himself in earlier and traveled down a series of winding tunnels leading to a broad subterranean expanse. Strapped down on his back and paraded around, Cyan could not help but feel like this was his funeral procession. He was due for one anyway.

The chatter all around fell to muffled whispers as they crossed the open chamber. He heard plenty, but saw nothing—all he could see was the cave ceiling.

They stopped. He craned his head up to look forward. The older lizard pulled open a massive iron door. The younger two carted Cyan in and dropped him on his face. He screamed in pain—he was sure he'd broken his nose again.

The lizards pressed their weight against the back of the cot, crushing Cyan into the floor. They undid his restraints hurriedly then retreated back through the door and shut it before he could get on his feet.

He was alone.

XVI

Cyan stooped, hands on his thighs, to settle himself. Then he put both hands on his face and reset his nose. A scream tore from his mouth as he worked his nose back into place. With all the times he'd died, he would have preferred dying to having to reset his broken nose. It hurt that much.

The inside of the shrine was as quiet as a tomb. Heavy stone bricks formed the walls, and cut into them were tall alcoves in the shape of windows, upon which were painted the same scenes he had noticed in all the other shrines he had visited. Free-floating fireballs hovered above his head to light the alcoves as well as the central path he walked along.

At the end of the path was another set of doors. He pulled them open and was immediately greeted with a blast of hot air and light that rushed out of the shrine's heart. He staggered backward, shielding his face with his arms. A glowing lava pool occupied the far half of the room. The molten rock bubbled, surged out of the pit and gushed onto the floor, and Cyan, panicked, turned to run.

"Hold," said the voice.

He stopped in place two paces from where he'd started.

"Why are you here, Cyan of Nordon?" rumbled a baritone voice from everywhere at once. Cyan leapt at the sound of it. It was bigger and deeper than the biggest thing he could think of, bigger even than the moon, if he had to guess.

Cyan turned around and saw that the lava had taken the shape of the fire dragon. His massive body was stocky and muscular. In size, he easily dwarfed the other dragons. He had limbs the size of ancient tree trunks and row upon row of horns crowning the peak of his head. The fires burning all over his body slowly died down and extinguished, revealing his red and orange scaled hide.

"Well?" the dragon asked. The faintest note of a growl underscored that word.

Cyan reached for his ax by instinct, and could have kicked himself for forgetting he didn't have it on him. "I've come for your medal."

"Is that so?" asked the dragon, plodding forward. The shrine rumbled with each step. He stopped and craned his neck down, putting his massive head — and array of fangs — inches from Cyan's face. "I thought as much. That's why I live beneath a volcano, you see. When I used to have visitors, mostly everyone who'd come to see me would challenge me for the medal."

He ran his talons down the shrine wall. Deep gouges opened in the rock. The dragon's talons were murderously sharp.

"That gets tedious quick," the dragon went on.

"I take it you are Hasaq."

The dragon bowed his head. "Indeed. But you did not come to make idle chatter. What makes you think I'll give you my medal?"

"Because I need it."

"How presumptuous of you," Hasaq said in a patronizing tone. "But I'm not surprised."

"Malaya and Imhra have already given me theirs," he said, holding up his bracer. "Fandi is just about convinced she'll lend me hers too. Give me yours and I'll be on my way."

"That isn't happening."

A sinister rumble emerged from the pit of the dragon's gullet. Cyan surmised this was the closest Hasaq got to a laugh.

"You will never leave this mountain," Hasaq said.

Cyan's blood went cold.

"You wandered someplace you didn't belong," Hasaq explained. "Terlu found you. You are Terlu's property now."

"I am no one's property."

"So you say. But that is not the way things work down here. If you will not submit, you will be incinerated. That is the law."

This time, it was Cyan who laughed. Much as he was in the right, it was a sad laugh, one that spoke of how badly he wanted to be proven wrong.

"You can't kill me," Cyan said with a tired grin. "I can't die."

"So I heard," Hasaq replied. "Which only means you will wish you could."

The force of the dragon's words struck Cyan like a mallet. If there were worse things than dying, then not dying while forever engulfed in flames was among them.

"Leave me and go to Terlu," said Hasaq.

"No," Cyan responded, his hands balled into angry fists. "Not until you give me what I came for."

Hasaq's laughter came off like the rattle of a venomous snake. "If you want my medal so badly, then take it." The dragon held up a forelimb and a smoldering fireball ignited in the air above his claw. The fires wisped away, revealing a bright red stone disk. No sooner had he called it into existence than he flung it into the lava pool behind him. It upended and sank to just beneath the surface of the molten rock, the tiniest bit of the medal peeking out from under the glowing magma.

"Go on," said Hasaq.

Cyan glared at the dragon with hate roiling in his eyes. He tramped off to the lava pool but stopped a few paces short. The light seared his eyes, the heat instantly squeezed beads of sweat from his pores. The air around the pit was unbearably hot.

"What's the matter?" Hasaq goaded him. "Too hot for you?"

Gritting his teeth, Cyan inched toward the lava pool. The metal on his body glowed ruddy orange, scalding his insides. The prize was within reach, floating just beneath the surface. Groaning with pain, he formed a pincer with his forefinger and thumb to pluck the medal out and reached an arm over the edge of the magma.

His arm burst into flames from fingers to shoulder. The fire spread to Cyan's hair and he screamed, losing himself in the moment. His arm thrashed into the magma, searing it cleanly off at the elbow. He flopped backward onto the floor, screaming, clutching his stump of an arm.

Hasaq shook his head at this. "I hadn't expected you to go ahead with that. Your greed really knows no ends." He plodded over to Cyan and craned his head down, level to his. "You fool. You will die from your injuries. Still, it would not be right to let you suffer needlessly." He pulled back a forelimb and balled his claw into a fist.

"No-no-no!" Cyan hardly had time to say as the massive dragon's fist came crashing down onto his head, crushing it like a grape.

* * *

Intact and with blood boiling, Cyan kicked up to his feet, much to the surprise of a very alarmed Hasaq. The dragon wheeled in place, his tail whipping around him.

"What kind of monster are you?" the dragon demanded.

Cyan thrust his gnashed teeth at him. A fine spray of spittle streaked through the air. Crouched on all fours, Cyan tore at the ground, closing the distance to Hasaq. The dragon swept his forearm into Cyan's path, knocking him aside and sending him somersaulting across the floor. His massive claw descended upon Cyan's back, pinning him down. Much though Cyan thrashed, he could not wriggle free of the hold.

"How did you do that?" asked Hasaq, his curiosity genuinely piqued.

Cyan answered with guttural snarls.

"My patience grows thin," Hasaq said, pressing down a little harder on Cyan's body. Cyan yelped in pain. "Answer me, or I will toss you into the flames."

It took all of his focus, but the rational part of Cyan's mind slowly came to the fore. "Curse!" he spat out before Hasaq could crush him flat.

The dragon let up slightly. "Explain."

"When I die, the armor brings me back."

"Intriguing," the dragon said under his breath. "I want it."

"I can't take it off. It's fused to me."

"A shame," said Hasaq. "Then I'll just have to pry it off you."

"No! There's another way!"

Hasaq paused a beat. "Go on."

"The only way I can take it off is by collecting the four medals of the elements," Cyan explained. "I have Malaya's and Imhra's. Soon I will have Fandi's as well."

"Yes, you said that earlier," the dragon snapped. "Did they test you beforehand?"

"No," Cyan lied.

"Really?" Hasaq pressed down on the claw crushing Cyan flat.

"Yes! Yes they did!"

The dragon gave a tired sigh. "I suppose I should too, then." He lifted his claw so Cyan could stand up. "Listen closely. For as long as my children have existed, I have cared for them here. They have everything in abundance under the mountain, except water. Their supply comes from the river at the foothills."

Hasaq paced away. "Except that they don't go to the river. Their water comes from below the earth, further down than where we stand now. Using my powers, I would heat the subterranean pools until the water came surging up, into their basin. But, over time, the soil below us has shifted. The water is now too far down to draw up, except with tremendous force, and doing so would collapse the tunnels my children call home. They all would die."

"I see," Cyan remarked, taking in all the details. "And so is this your test?"

"It is."

"Then the answer is simple: let them go to the river and get water."

The dragon shook his massive head. "They can't. They cannot live outside of the mountain."

The dragon's face set into a hard look. "I shall grant you five days' time to arrive at a solution to our water problem."

Cyan was about to interject and to say that five days was not long enough to produce an answer, but Hasaq raised his voice the minute he saw Cyan's mouth open.

"Additionally," said Hasaq, "I will allow you to leave Mount Kierns to seek help elsewhere. If you are unsuccessful by noon on the fifth day, then you are not worthy to possess my emblem."

Cyan resolved right then, that if there was any doubt he would not succeed by the fifth day, he would put a few leagues of distance between himself and Mount Kierns.

"Don't think of fleeing, either," Hasaq said.

Cyan blanched.

The dragon scowled. "If you run, I will find you, and what will await you will be worse than anything you can imagine."

The warrior swallowed hard.

"Go now," Hasaq said, turning around to climb back into the lava. "My children are dying. They won't last very long." The dragon eased into the fire pit. The magma accepted him so gently that the pool did not even bubble as the huge dragon became one with the flames.

XVII

With Terlu as his guide, Cyan traversed the network of caves within the mountain. They arrived at a massive cylindrical room within which was erected a cistern hewn from solid rock. The lizardfolk were thronged in the room in tight lines—while the community was not very large, to Cyan it seemed as though the entire population was present. Terlu pushed past the lines and Cyan followed her.

"This is our water supply," Terlu said, slowing her pace so Cyan could catch up. "When Father Hasaq wills it, water surges up from vents in the ground at the bottom of the basin."

Cyan followed Terlu up the steps built into the side of the reservoir. He peered over its edge. There was a lot of open air within the basin, and not much water. The basin was fifty feet deep, at least to the level of water below.

"I noticed that you have the medal of water," Terlu said.

He raised an eyebrow.

"Father Hasaq told us about the medals before. Perhaps you can use yours to fill our basin with water."

"If you concede that I'm no longer your property."

"Yes," she said without a moment's hesitation.

"Very well." He shut his eyes and focused his will, gathering energy from the medal into his body to expend on creating water in the basin. When he opened his eyes he was shocked to find that absolutely nothing had happened.

"Use the medal of water to refill our basin," said Terlu.

"I'm trying," he said, palpably annoyed. He shut his eyes again, concentrating harder this time. A single bubble broke the surface of the water in the cistern.

Seeing as this was getting him nowhere, Cyan climbed down to the ground level with Terlu close behind.

"Give me a second," he said. He concentrated and whispered Imhra's name.

For a while nothing happened. Then, after several tense moments, wisps of vapor began to emerge from the cistern. Gradually the vapor took the form of the water dragon, and Imhra appeared before them both, hovering over the mouth of the basin.

Terlu, astounded, threw herself to the floor out of humility. The packed mass of lizardfolk watched wide-eyed, dumbfounded, then all bowed low at once as though choreographed.

"Please, get up," Imhra addressed them. "There's no need for that." Then turning to Cyan, "What can I do for you?"

"Imhra," Cyan said, "these creatures have asked me to refill their water supply, yet my powers fail me here. Would you know why this is?"

"Yes. It's the same reason why it took me so long to get here—you can't work with what you don't have."

"I don't understand."

"There is a water reservoir down below, but it's trapped in the rock. Almost nothing gets through the cracks except for some steam. Since it's so far down, your powers cannot agitate the water enough for it to flow up the vents leading here. In fact, not even I alone could do that."

"Are you saying we will have no more water?" Terlu asked.

Imhra remained silent, preferring not to admit the truth.

"There has got to be a way to free that water so it flows up here," Cyan said. "Do you think Malaya might be of help?"

"It's worth a try."

Terlu leaned over and whispered in Cyan's ear, "You must be very fortunate to be able to call such powerful beings your friends."

159

"He had to work hard to earn our trust," said Imhra, having overheard what she said.

Cyan called out the earth dragon's name, and a mound of stone and earth immediately rose up from the ground before them. The soil and rocks streamed off the green dragon's scales and he shook himself clean. The lizardfolk dove to the floor in unison.

"Hello, Imhra," Malaya said. "What trouble is Cyan in that he needs the both of us to get him out?"

"Malaya," Cyan began, "the residents of this community have given me the task of refilling their water supply, but neither the medal of water nor Imhra herself can do this."

"How does this involve me?"

"We know that there is water below the surface but it is trapped down below. I was hoping you would be able to release the water so these creatures do not die of thirst."

Malaya nodded. "How very unlike you to think of others for a change. This makes me regret lending you my medal a bit less." His face went stoic. "You are correct, there is a considerable amount of water below us. However, I fear that if I try to release the water, it might run further down into the earth where it will be lost. Alternatively, freeing the water might collapse these tunnels." He paused. "I'm fairly certain you don't want that."

Imhra frowned. "It looks like we can't be of much help to you, Cyan."

Hand at his chin, Cyan sifted his mind for the glimmer of an idea. "Malaya, I need to you run some reconnaissance on the layout of Mount Kierns. Burrow through the mountain and get me a cross-sectional map. And be careful," he stressed. "We don't want the whole place collapsing on itself."

"That I can do," said Malaya.

Cyan turned to Imhra. "Meet me at the wind shrine in a few minutes," he said, gripping his wind charm.

XVIII

Cyan landed in the same mud hole directly beneath the wind shrine, except today it was not raining and the depression in the ground was dry. His ax came hurtling down like a comet, narrowly missing his ear. He stood up and called on Imhra.

She appeared before him in seconds. "That was quick. I take it you need me to get you up there again."

He nodded.

"Okay, you know what to do," she said, leaning forward so he could climb up. The warrior climbed onto her neck and Imhra took off, dropping him off at the doorstep of the shrine.

Cyan walked in, finding the place just the same as the last time he was there. Basp, perched just above the entrance on the inside, watched him with brooding eyes, his lance resting on his shoulder.

"You've returned," said the birdman, none too enthusiastically. "The mistress expects you. Follow me." He flew down from the ledge and escorted him to the opposite end of the shrine, then opened the door for him. Once the warrior was inside, a swift gale picked him up off his feet and carried him to the shrine's roof, where it gently set him down before the wind dragon.

Fandi lay on her back on the shrine's roof, sunning herself. "You're late. By a lot."

"I know. Some things happened to delay my coming," he admitted. "Have you decided whether I am worthy of your medal?"

"I have decided whether I should give you another chance."

"And?" he asked, dying to know but not wanting to sound hasty.

"The answer is yes."

"What will you have me do?"

"The task I have will be proof enough that you actually possess a noble bone in your body. At first glance it appears simple enough, but no doubt this request will demand every bit of your ingenuity and willpower. Are you ready?"

"Yes."

"We shall see," said Fandi. "A few days ago it came to my attention that a certain community is suffering from a water shortage…"

"Oh hell," Cyan griped. She did not have to say any more for him to know exactly what was going on. "Let me guess: Mount Kierns? I was just there…"

"So you're saying I need to think of something else?"

"No-no-no," said Cyan, putting out his arms. He let out his breath with a sigh. "That's a worthy task," he said, not sounding at all enthusiastic.

"I thought so," said Fandi, matter-of-factly.

"And if it's not too much to ask, could you spare me a wind charm?"

"I knew you'd ask me for one sooner or later." She snapped her talons and a tiny gold light began to glimmer in the air before Cyan. Swift gales billowed up, whirling into a vortex around the globe of light, collapsing it into a pinpoint before bursting with a flash.

At Cyan's feet lay a carved amber ring as big as the palm of his hand. A thin strand of golden cord passed through a loop in the charm. He tied a knot and hung the charm around his neck.

He cradled his chin with his hand and thought hard. "Any ideas on how I can solve the water problem?"

She shrugged her shoulders. "It's your task, not mine."

Cyan smirked. Fandi's attitude wasn't helping. "Thank you for giving me another chance."

"You're welcome," she said, not looking in his direction.

Seeing that he wouldn't get any further help from Fandi, Cyan clutched his new wind charm and envisioned the interior of the fire shrine.

Much to Cyan's relief, Fandi's charm was refreshingly more behaved than the one Wren had given him. In a heartbeat he was awash in yellow light. No sooner had it receded than he found himself within the fire shrine's heart, his ax obediently resting in the grip of his right hand.

Malaya sat comfortably in the corner, waiting for him.

"Good of you to show up when you did," said the dragon. "I have the information you need."

"Excellent," he responded. "Let's get started on this right away."

Malaya spread his arms and a slab of white granite popped into existence on the ground before him. He scored the granite with the tip of his talon, and the grooves filled with solid black as though they had been charred into the stone.

"This is Mount Kierns," Malaya said, drawing a large triangle. He added a horizontal line across the top third of the mountain, along with an intersecting vertical channel that rose up from deep below the mountain. "This top portion is the crater full of magma. The magma rises through this shaft I've drawn here."

He then drew a box halfway down the mountain, away from the lava vent. Directly below he drew a second box, much bigger and further down the mountain than the first. He placed an X within that box. "This first box is the strata where we now stand. Way down below is where the water lies."

"There's no getting at that water, is there?" Cyan asked.

"Not likely, and certainly not any time soon."

Malaya scored a curving line at the ground level of the diagram. "This line here is the river that runs alongside Mount Kierns."

The spark of an idea went off in Cyan's mind. He knelt close to the diagram for a better look. Rubbing his chin, he dropped the index finger of his other hand on the mountain and traced a straight line to the river. The river and the lizardfolk compound were on the same side of the mountain.

"What if we were to divert the river?" Cyan asked.

Malaya shifted his head to face Cyan.

"Here," Cyan said, pointing to the lizardfolk compound. "We'll have you burrow a channel into the side of the mountain." He traced a path through the mountainside. "The channel will lead from the river through the mountain, emptying into the reservoir."

Malaya stood quiet a moment, considering this. "I think this might just work."

XIX

Sunup the next morning saw Cyan and the four elemental dragons on the banks of the river. The first rays of morning peeked out from around the sides of the mountain, casting an orange glow partway up the purple sky. The preparations were set—Malaya had already dug the canal into the side of the mountain leading to the lizardfolk community's reservoir. The earth displaced in the tunneling had been piled up to form an embankment dam on the riverbank, erected to prevent the water from entering the channel prematurely.

Beaming a wide smile at his own genius, Cyan walked up alongside the dam and addressed the dragons.

"I'm very proud you all are here to witness this," said Cyan. "Those of you who already have placed your trust in me, thank you; and those of you who have yet to will soon find reason to do so."

Impatient smoke wisped out of Hasaq's nostrils. Seeing this, Cyan knew better than to press the issue further.

Cyan took a deep breath and held it, eyes shut, concentrating. He thrust out his left hand in a halting gesture and the river reared up like a startled horse. The water surged and crashed back onto itself, leaving the downstream riverbed dry. Then he thrust out his right hand, punching at the air between him and the embankment. The dam broke at its center in a burst of flying dirt.

He then lowered both arms. The river surged down its watercourse, forming a new rivulet as it filled the fresh channel into the mountain. The cheers echoing from down below gave proof that his plan was a complete success.

Imhra beamed a proud smile. "You did it!"

"I suppose you did," said Fandi, rolling her eyes. "Fair is fair."

She clenched her fist and a yellow wind spun into a tight vortex at her claw. It receded just as quickly, leaving only an amber disk. No sooner had it appeared than Cyan snatched it up and fused it into his bracer with the others.

Cyan turned to address Hasaq. Hasaq's shoulders were slumped and his head held low as though the mighty dragon were cowed.

"Sir Wraithwate," said Hasaq, demonstrating the most civility he had since meeting Cyan, "I do believe I owe you an apology. In truth, I owe you two."

"No need," Cyan said flatly.

"Please, let me finish," he answered, holding up a claw. "First, I did not think you were capable of fulfilling what you promised. Knowing what I do of your past, I figured you were unworthy of my trust." He sighed, and his great body heaved with a giant solemn breath. "Secondly, I must report that I have lent my powers to someone else."

Betrayed! Cyan's seething mind registered. His eyes widened, then narrowed sharply. He was on the verge of exploding with anger.

"Is... that... so?" he said through gritted teeth, buying time to swallow his bile.

"It is so," Hasaq said. "Like my colleagues, I cannot take back my emblem unless one uses its powers for ill. The current bearer of my trust has done no wrong, so he is as entitled as you to my powers."

"So will we share the medal?" Cyan asked.

"It cannot be shared. You must go to the one who possesses my emblem and take it from him if you wish to win it for yourself."

Cyan balled his hands into angry fists. "Show me to him. I'll rip that medal out of his hands."

Hasaq frowned. Mild disappointment registered collectively upon the dragons' faces.

"Are you sure you want to do this?" Hasaq asked.

"Show me to him."

"Very well. Brace yourself, warrior. This might be a little uncomfortable."

Suddenly Cyan's body became very hot, as though he had instantly developed a fever—except this was the strangest fever ever. Warmth radiated up from the soles of his feet, filling him utterly, up to his scalp before intensifying. He broke a sweat, and whether it was because of the heat or how nervous he felt, he could not tell.

"What's happening to me?" Cyan demanded.

"Just hold on a little longer," Hasaq responded.

Everything in his field of vision swayed as his eyeballs simmered in their sockets. The dragons became mere blotches. There was a burst of heat and a flash of flame, and he was gone, finding himself in a dank laboratory lit by row after row of dim candles.

An intense disorientation came over Cyan. His head spun. He sat on the ground with his ax in his lap. It took him several minutes to settle himself enough to try standing up.

"That's one way to make an entrance."

Cyan jerked his head in the direction of the voice. Standing in the doorframe with arms crossed was Wren, looking not the least bit amused.

"If I had known you were coming I'd have made tea," the wizard went on.

Cyan braced the shaft of his ax against the floor and stood. "Where is it?"

"Tsk-tsk," Wren chided. "Not so much as a 'hello'. To answer your question, I have it."

"I'm not here to play games, wizard," Cyan seethed. "You don't know what I've been through. What you've put me through."

Wren's arms swung to his sides. "Fine." He dug into his pocket and held up a bright red disk Cyan knew had to be the fire medal.

It was no small surprise to learn Wren possessed the medal of fire. With all that Cyan had had to endure just to get this far, he could not imagine what Wren must have been put through. He smirked inwardly. "What test did the dragon put you to beforehand?"

"None."

Cyan's jaw dropped in exasperation. "But I... How?"

"I sought it purely for academic reasons," Wren cut him short. "And besides, compared to you I'm a saint." He paused. "There is something I need to tell you first. I've come to learn that the four medals alone will not raise your curse..."

"What?" Cyan shouted. His hands choked up on his ax.

"But there is a power behind them that will."

"Go on," muttered Cyan.

"The medals are powerful in their own right, but ultimately, they are keys to a far greater power. It is only by tapping into this greater power that you may be freed of your curse."

Arms crossed, Cyan stood silent, listening intently to every word. "So you're sending me out on another quest?" He sighed with the weariness of one who has grown tired of life. "Fine, wizard. What must I do now?"

"I don't know."

Cyan's eyes narrowed.

"I'm not through researching," Wren finished.

"How much longer will you need?"

The wizard smiled, and Cyan got a sinking feeling. "Only as long as it takes for you to take this medal," said Wren.

Cyan closed on Wren with an arm extended, but stopped short of reaching for the medal.

"Wait," he said. "How did you get it before me?"

"I've had it all this time."

"I don't believe that for a minute. If you'd had it all this time, you would have given it to me at the outset."

"You never asked me for it."

Cyan frowned. Wren had a point there. "How was I supposed to know?"

The wizard shrugged his shoulders. "So, do you want it or not?"

Scowling, Cyan snatched the medal from Wren's outstretched hand and fused it into his bracer. All four medals began to glow their respective colors, filling the room with green, blue, yellow, and red light. Cyan was struck blind that instant, then a misty starfield of blue and black swept across his mind's eye. A strange word echoed clearly in Cyan's head in a voice that was not his own.

"Omedajeron," he said it out loud.

"Omedajeron!" Wren said, pumping a fist. "Well done. Shut your eyes now and say it with every fiber of your being."

Wren did not have to tell him, as Cyan was already preparing to do as bidden. A mystic wind filled his lungs near to the point of bursting and he screamed the word louder than any man had ever yelled. The next thing he knew, he was catapulting across time and space. Passing stars blurred into solid streaks, coming on faster and faster until everything he saw was light, then nothing.

XX

He had arrived at a secret place beyond mortal reach. Cyan and Wren stood on a pale marble walkway floating in the middle of an inky black starfield. The cosmos swirled all around them; comets streaked across the cobalt-black expanse of infinity. Stars winked gently from all around, welcoming the newcomers with soft white light.

"Where are we?" Cyan asked breathlessly.

"Omedajeron, where else?" Wren answered in a matter-of-fact tone.

"What's that mean, wizard?"

Wren balked at having to explain the obvious. "The end of time, the middle of nowhere — what difference does it make?" His voice was giddy with a dangerous undercurrent. "What matters is that we're here!"

"Wherever here is," Cyan said under his breath.

Wren paced down the marble walkway, looking all around. "It's beautiful, really. Have you ever seen such majesty? Such beauty of design?"

Cyan was hard pressed to disagree. This place was unlike anything mortals were ever meant to experience, probably because they weren't meant to venture there. He could not understand the place and frankly, it scared the daylights out of him. Everything about it betrayed the laws of the physical world. He craned his neck up to track the path of a blue planet that drifted far above them, cruising slowly from right to left.

"Come, Cyan," said Wren, marching down the path.

At the end of a walkway was a platform that swept wide like an amphitheater's stage. Standing at the very center of the platform was what looked like a monstrous pair of hooked ivory tusks. The tusks were set into the ground with their widest ends down, their points in the air, facing each other. It vaguely resembled a door, except there was nothing but empty space between the two.

Cyan approached and noticed a silver plate set in the ground before the tusk archway. Etched into the plate was a pattern of four circles connected by narrow grooves. Wren knelt before the plate and beckoned for Cyan to draw nearer.

"Hold your bracer against the plate," said Wren. "Fit the medals into the slots."

Cyan got on his knees and pressed his forearm against the plate in the ground. The four elemental emblems instantly melted into a runny gel, pouring into the slots carved in the panel. They solidified again just as quickly.

The archway suddenly came to life, casting an oppressive purple glow. He backed away from the panel and watched as the once empty space within the portal became opaque.

"Come, warrior," Wren instructed, before stepping through the arch and disappearing entirely from view.

Cyan steeled himself, put a hand through the portal and whipped it back out. Half-convinced that the portal would do him no harm, he stepped inside and was engulfed in black.

He could see nothing.

There was nothing.

Cyan was nothing.

He blinked — or at least he thought he had, if indeed his eyes were open — and then again, and could see as well as though his eyes were shut. He lost his sense of place right then and let his breath out just to see if he could hear it — if he could hear it, he still existed — and before he knew it he was hyperventilating. His heart raced. This was cold comfort, but at least it was a sign he was still alive.

"Wren?" Cyan called out.

"What?" he answered. It had been a delay of but a second, but still too long for Cyan's liking.

A pair of blue fires, one to either side of them, lit up ten feet from where they stood. Then another pair, and another in rapid succession, each coming faster than the first. A string of blue fires shot away into the distance, tracking two perfectly straight lines. By the dim light they cast, Cyan could just barely make out the double doors at the end of the line of flames.

"Onward," Wren said, and they walked to the doors.

Cyan readied his ax. "The layout of this place seems oddly familiar."

"It ought to. You've visited several dragon shrines, and this is one of them."

Cyan swallowed hard. Considering that this place was more bizarre than anything he could ever dream up, he could not imagine how formidable this shrine's guardian would have to be.

"Put your ax away," said Wren. "You needn't fear a guardian. The dragon in the chamber ahead has more power in the tip of his shortest talon than anything your brutish warrior mind can conceive."

"Will he test us?"

"Oh yes."

Cyan frowned.

They reached end of the walkway, where a pair of double doors stood in the middle of a raised marble dais. The doors were shut, but if they were designed to keep things out, they failed at that terribly. The doorframe was not set into a wall—there were no walls, anywhere, it seemed—rather, the doors were built as a freestanding structure. He paced up to the doors, then around them to their other side, and back around until he got to where he started.

"What foolishness is this?" Cyan asked.

"It's a door, Cyan."

"I know that!" he snapped, sick of the wizard's patronizing. "It goes nowhere."

"Not so," said Wren, holding up an index finger to make his point. "It leads to the inner sanctum." He put his hand on the door's brass ring and went to open it. Cyan clasped his wrist, stopping him cold.

"If the dragon beyond this door is as powerful as you say, he'll make short work of you," Cyan said. "Maybe that's a good thing in itself, but I'll need you to get me back home."

Wren's brow furrowed. "You cannot deal with this dragon the same way you did with the others. It would be better for us if I went in first, and then I let you in afterward."

Cyan drilled a hard look into Wren's face, then let him go with a shove. "No tricks, wizard."

Wren nodded, then opened the door and stepped inside, closing the door behind him.

Cyan waited, pacing in front of the door for what seemed like an eternity. Intermittently he pressed his ear to the door to see if he could hear anything happening inside. Silence. He backed away and paced some more.

The door lurched open a crack, snagging his attention.

"Enter, Cyan," Wren's voice called out from within.

Ax in hand, he pulled the door open and walked into the shrine's heart. Before him stood Wren alongside a dragon as black a moonless night. His jaw dropped upon seeing the sheer size of the creature. Easily four times as big as hulking Hasaq, the massive dark-scaled master of the shrine watched him with eyes the size of full moons and just as bright.

"I do humbly greet you, Cyan Wraithwate of Nordon," the dragon said in a smooth, deep voice that reverberated overwhelming power and wisdom. "I am Usra."

Cyan staggered in a few paces. His ax fell from his numb hands. He craned his neck back to meet the massive dragon's gaze.

"I am informed you have come to me seeking to be freed of a curse," the dragon said. "It is my great pleasure to be of service."

With just those words the armor pieces fell from Cyan's body, clattering noisily on the floor. They let up steam, then melted into puddles of blood that bubbled and evaporated away into mist. Cyan smiled ear to ear, then laughed despite himself. He grabbed his arm, then his hand and fingers, and then felt his thighs and legs to make certain what he saw was not just a cruel joke. Only the bracer remained on his arm, fastened securely but not forged into his skin. He tore the buckles off and hurled it to the ground.

"Better now, Cyan?" asked Wren.

Cyan thought to grace him with a smile and nod, but decided upon just the nod. After all, it was all Wren's fault that he had to undergo such a misadventure. He felt Wren didn't deserve the smile.

"Good," Wren said. "Fair is fair. You got what you wanted out of this. As did I."

Cyan did not like the way he had said that. "Explain."

"Him." Wren pointed to the hulking figure beside him. "Usra oversees time and space, all that is and all that isn't." His smile widened to show teeth. "And he does what I tell him to."

Cyan's brow knit. This all was coming faster than he could process. "You..." he stammered. "You tricked me!" He turned to the dragon. "I also have earned a share of your power. Getting here alone merits that."

The dragon frowned sullenly. "I cannot grant that request."

"Then I'll change my wish. Take back that you freed me from the cursed armor."

"I am sorry," said the dragon.

Wren snickered. "It was never your wish to begin with. It was mine."

"This is true," said Usra. "He was the first to reach me."

Cyan's heart raced madly, beating against his chest as though fighting to be let out. He snapped his ax up from the ground.

"You cheated me!" Cyan yelled.

"That is some way to show your thanks. I freed you of your curse, and you accuse me of being unfair? Tsk-tsk." Wren shook his head. "Not that it matters. Destiny awaits us both, and yours is to die. Permanently, this time." He faced the dragon. "Kill him."

The dragon inhaled deeply, swelling his chest with air. He let fly a surging jet of bluish-purple fire from his jaws. Cyan dove out of the way as the wave of wickedly intense flame surged through the air. He hit the ground and rolled to his feet in a smooth motion, one hand on the ground for support, his eyes on the dragon watching for his next move but knowing he was only prolonging the inevitable. There was no way he could defeat this creature. An army of men would have a hard time putting the dragon down.

The dragon's eyes flashed with rage. He inhaled again, deeper than before, and released a sweeping stream of dark fire, dousing the chamber in flames as he swung his head from side to side. A solid wall of flames rushed toward Cyan. There was no escape this time. He threw up his arms to block his face as the fire washed over him.

* * *

The next thing Cyan knew he was standing before the lava pit at the heart of Hasaq's shrine, not sure how he got there but thankful nonetheless. The fire dragon stood in a corner. The other dragons were arrayed beside him.

"How…" Cyan stammered. "Why am I here?"

"I saw it all," Hasaq said. "I was with you the whole time."

A somber look crossed the dragon's face. The others looked just as despondent.

"Cyan, listen," said Hasaq. "Time is short and the situation is not good. Evil has come to Omedajeron. Everything hangs in the balance."

Cyan was about to ask what he meant by that when Hasaq cut him off.

"Everything," the dragon stressed, indicating he intended that word to mean nothing short of all it stood for. "We, as the keepers of the balance, are obligated to contain this evil. We four have already recalled our powers, but that alone means nothing now. We need a champion, one who will go in our name to put an end to this threat."

Cyan raised an eyebrow.

"I nominate Cyan Wraithwate as my champion," said Hasaq.

"But…" Cyan interjected.

"I nominate Cyan Wraithwaite," said Imhra.

"I nominate Cyan Wraithwaite," said Fandi.

"I nominate Cyan Wraithwaite," said Malaya.

"It is unanimous. Then it shall be so," Hasaq went on. "As long as our candidate also wishes it."

They watched him with pleading eyes. To see such great beasts cowed instilled in Cyan that whatever threat loomed was no trivial thing. And yet, to have these four come to him with such a heavy responsibility spoke of their trust in him.

"Will you be our champion?" asked Hasaq.

He was taken aback. "Why me?"

"Because we trust you," said Malaya.

"We all had our doubts about you at first," Imhra said. "You were as evil and self-centered a man as they come."

Fandi spoke next. "In fulfilling the quests we gave you, you showed us you weren't so bad that you couldn't change."

"You understand now that this is no small thing we ask of you," Hasaq said. "We will not impose a burden you are unwilling to carry."

"But," said Imhra, "if you do agree to be our champion, you will not go alone. We shall entrust our powers to you."

"But I left the medals back at the gateway," Cyan said.

"The medals are only representations of our power," said Malaya. "They mean nothing in and of themselves."

"Decide quickly," said Hasaq with mounting impatience. "Yes or no — will you be our champion?"

The dragons bored into him with their stares. Cyan's eyes darted from one dragon to the other. This was altogether too much to take in, and coming too fast for comfort. Was he truly worthy, or even capable of carrying out the task laid before him? He wasn't sure. But, there was only one way to find out.

"I accept," he said at last. "But for my purposes and not yours. I go because that bastard Wren needs to be taught a lesson."

"Very well," said Hasaq.

The dragons encircled the warrior, shut their eyes and began meditating.

Standing at the center, Cyan could feel invisible waves of energy washing over him. Every hair on his body stood on end. The dragons began to glow and emit wisps of their respective colors. A thunderbolt surged from Malaya's body and into Cyan's, linking the two with an arc of light and heat. A bolt shot from Imhra, then from Fandi, and finally Hasaq.

Cyan's body was consumed by fire that did not burn; his skin turned to rock; a swirling gale howled all around him; torrential rain poured down from above.

A thunderclap tore the air. It was over as abruptly as it had come on. Cyan collapsed to his knees, then sat back on his haunches, utterly spent.

"Cyan," Hasaq said.

The warrior raised his head just enough to acknowledge him.

"Our strength is with you," he went on. "We trust you will do the right thing."

The room sheared apart into runny streaks of color as he was zipped away in a flash of light.

XXI

Seeing only red through eyes made narrow by spite, Cyan walked to the heart of the shrine with a knuckle-whitening grip on his ax. The door gave way to a hearty push and opened before him, and there stood Wren and the dragon.

"You were a fool to return," said Wren. "I know not how you escaped last time, but you will not be so lucky twice."

"Let's see if when I'm through with you there's enough to feed to the birds," Cyan shot back.

Wren turned to face the dragon.

"Hey!" Cyan called out, drawing Wren's attention. "Fight your own battles, coward! Don't sick your pet dragon on me."

The wizard smirked. "Were you in my place, you'd do the same." He pointed at Cyan. "Kill him."

The dragon crouched low on all fours, snarling, its lips pulled back to bare its fearsome array of jagged teeth. As he bore down on Cyan, Cyan leapt straight up with a conjured updraft at his feet. He soared into the air as the dragon pounced just beneath him, landing heavily on the spot where he stood. At the apex of his leap Cyan thrust out his hand and launched an arcing gout of flame from his palm, aimed for Wren. It was upon the wizard in moments—in a heartbeat, Wren leapt aside as the flame burst into a globe of flash heat, charring the ground black. Cyan landed just after, ax primed for a sweep at the wizard's neck, but caught nothing but empty air.

The ground trembled beneath his feet. Cyan spun in place in time to spy the dragon's charge. In mid-stride the black dragon reared his head back and breathed a surge of purple flames. Cyan ran toward the flames, hurling himself headlong, at the last minute slicking the floor ahead of him with a thin layer of ice. He coasted between the dragon's legs and across the length of the chamber, coming to an abrupt stop where the trail of ice ended.

He sprang to his feet and no sooner had he done so than blinding pain wracked his body, dropping him to his knees. Lightning surged all over his body, curling his fingers into hooks. Each jolt came on like a thousand hot needles jabbed in his skin. His body jerked and danced—he was a puppet, lightning was his strings, and pulling the strings was Wren. Even over the sound of his own screams, Cyan could hear Wren laughing.

At just that moment Cyan pictured the hardest stone he could think of. His body stiffened, lost pliability as his flesh become granite. It was a bizarre feeling, but it beat being subjected to more of Wren's lightning. A frustrated grimace crossed the wizard's face as he pumped his arms harder, each time sending a stronger bolt careening toward Cyan.

Cyan took a ponderous step forward. His body had become several times heavier. It was slow-going, but he paced away toward his ax and swept it up into his eager hands.

The dragon charged him again, spewing a blast of blinding purple flames. Nicks and chips flew off Cyan's granite body between the relentless gout of fire and bursts of lightning. Cyan put his head down and pressed through it all, timing his advance. Just as the dragon was upon him, he let fly a mighty uppercut stroke. Cyan's ax halted the dragon's charge and reared him up on his hind legs as the blade bit deep into his scales. The dragon split open from his belly to his throat, staggered backward and toppled over.

"A minor setback," the dragon said, slowly getting to his feet.

Cyan wasted no time in decapitating the dragon in one swift stroke. He fed the momentum of his swing into a chain of sweeping strikes, lopping off a forelimb and the opposite claw in rapid succession. That would buy him some time, or so Cyan hoped.

"You can't kill him," said Wren. A resolute look burned in the wizard's eyes as Cyan hacked the

191

dragon to pieces, but in that look, hidden away in the back, was a twinge of horror.

"It's not him I want dead," Cyan replied with a wicked smile.

The wizard swallowed hard.

Cyan broke into a run, his skin reverting to flesh in mid-stride. The weight of his stone body fell away and he was upon Wren frighteningly quick. Wren darted aside as the ax came down. Cyan's ax struck the ground with a peal of metal on stone, knocking sparks from the floor. Wren's scream pierced through the ringing steel. He drew back, clutching his arm.

Cyan hefted his ax. The blade was spattered in blood. On the floor was Wren's right arm, severed at the elbow.

"You... bastard!" Wren shouted, cradling his wounded arm. He backed away as Cyan closed on him.

Once he was in striking distance, Cyan brought up his foot and kicked Wren in the chest, knocking him onto his backside. Then, with a satisfied grin, he adjusted his grip and raised his ax over his head for a finishing stroke.

Wren's hand shot forward and hurled a shower of white sparks. Cyan's body jerked as the sparks drove into his chest. The white-hot sheen cooled into shards of jagged metal.

"Ugh," Cyan sputtered, his body listing to one side with the weight of his ax. He teetered on unsteady feet, then with his last ounce of strength nudged the ax over the top of its center of mass. He did not so much swing it down as merely hold on to it as it fell, burying itself deeply into Wren's sprawled body. Wren died instantly, cleft in two by the mighty stroke. As the searing pain came on, Cyan almost wished he had, too.

He fell onto his haunches and rolled onto his side. The jagged metal dug deeper into him with each movement, each breath, each heartbeat.

He coughed, and it ached to his core. Blood spilled from his lips. He could feel death coming, and he knew what that felt like, having experienced it so often. Fear shot though him that moment. He was going to die and there would be no coming back this time, difficult as that was to believe. He almost welcomed it. His heavy eyelids closed.

"You don't have to die," Usra's baritone voice rang out in his head.

The suddenness of his having spoken popped Cyan's eyes open. The dragon stood before him, watching him with his enormous glowing eyes. Lying on the ground just within reach was the bracer.

"Not if you don't want to," the dragon went on.

The bracer lay with its straps undone and its recessed area facing upward. Even with what little strength Cyan had left, it would be an easy thing to raise his forearm and let it fall into the armor piece. The bracer would do the rest of the work itself.

"Think about it," said the dragon.

There was a burst of light in his mind's eye, then images in rapid succession. An imposing man fully clad in armor held aloft the red pennant of battle. He stood on a high peak. Below him, the land ran to the horizons, a patchwork of cities, hamlets, castles and farms.

The pennant flapped as though caught in a stiff wind, growing to envelop everything it came across, covering the land from end to end.

The man in armor raised his weapon in triumph. There was no way of knowing who the man in armor was, but Cyan noted that the ax he held looked markedly familiar.

The vision cut out with a jolt.

"A kingdom, a continent, a world," said Usra. "Your pennant will fly in every nation over every people. What say you, Cyan?"

A breathy whisper left Cyan's mouth as his lips moved to form words. "I…" he said, extending an arm. "I… want…"

"You want it?" said the dragon, nudging the bracer closer.

"I… want… to die," he said as his breath left him. He rolled over onto his back with his arm still extended. The last thing he ever saw was him raising the middle finger to the dragon and his bracer.

It was massively satisfying.

* * *

"Well, hello."

Cyan whirled in place at the sound of that voice, his hands clenched into fists.

"Again," said Wren. He descended a white marble staircase and stopped short a few paces from Cyan.

"You!" Cyan yelled. He ran at Wren with an arm cocked to lay him out. When he got within striking distance he launched his fist at the wizard's face. The momentum carried him head over heels, dropping him squarely onto his backside. He had missed.

"Calm down," said Wren, coming up behind him. "There's no need for that."

Cyan stood. "Damn it! How many times do I have to kill you?"

"How many times have you died?"

"Answer me!" Cyan roared.

Wren hesitated. "You don't have to kill me. You never had to."

"You deserved it anyway."

Wren gave a tired smile. "Perhaps." Fingers knit at his breast, he paced away. "I'm glad you made it here."

What he said made Cyan take pause. All at once a feeling of intense disorientation came over him. He glanced up and around, and over his shoulder. He was in a palace foyer tiled in white marble. Pillars soared on either side of a grand double staircase leading up to a gleaming white mezzanine. If it all weren't so beautiful, it would be difficult to look at from the sheen coming off the impeccable surfaces.

"Where am I?" Cyan asked.

Wren chuckled. "Take a guess."

Cyan's eyes got huge as the weight of that short phrase set in. "That doesn't make sense. I killed you."

"And you died."

"So that means…"

Wren nodded.

"But how are you—am I—here? You were going to do something terrible…"

"Do what, exactly?"

That was Hasaq's voice. Cyan spun in place and there stood the hulking red dragon. Even he looked smaller within the cavernous foyer.

Cyan opened his mouth to respond, but found that he didn't have an answer. After giving it some thought, he realized that he never was told what catastrophe Wren might cause if he didn't stop him in time—nor was he told that Wren was the one who would work that evil in the first place.

"Remember when I said evil had arrived at Omedajeron?" Hasaq went on. "I meant you."

Cyan's jaw dropped.

"Omedajeron was your final test," Hasaq explained. "Granted, your intentions for going back weren't the purest."

Terlu stepped out from behind Hasaq. "Ultimately, you resisted the final temptation, and you've shown that you're not as bad a person as we first thought," she said.

"You had a few rough patches, though." It was Imhra who spoke. Alongside her were Eleanor and her father.

Eleanor leveled her angry eyes on Cyan; her father crossed his arms and shot a disapproving look his way. Despite himself, Cyan felt very ashamed. It was a feeling he was not used to.

Malaya appeared from the far corner, seemingly out of nowhere. "You learned to be patient, not to jump to conclusions, not to judge others too quickly, and that it's all right to not always get your way."

"Also," said Fandi, "you learned to trust others."

Cyan hung his head. "I'm really very sorry for all I've done."

"There's no need for that," said Wren, and just then Terlu, Eleanor and her father vanished in bursts of light. "You see, none of this actually ever happened."

Cyan's breath left him in rasps. "What?"

The dragons vanished in a concussive flash, leaving only Wren and Cyan.

"Well," Wren corrected himself, "it all did happen, in a way. It was real enough. Your quest gave you ample opportunity to change your ways. If you hadn't, you surely would have been doomed. But as we stand here right now, neither you nor I exist—rather, you existed, once. I exist, but I'm not really what you see."

"You're not making any sense," Cyan said through clenched teeth.

"I'll admit, it's difficult to explain," said Wren. "But it all boils down to this: you got a second chance. You sure didn't deserve it, but you got one because you had the potential to redeem yourself. Not everyone is so lucky."

Cyan's knees wobbled and gave out. They folded in on themselves, dropping him onto his backside. All at once, each of his shortcomings—every single selfish, callous, and coldhearted deed he'd committed, ever—flashed in his mind's eye. Shame burned under his skin so powerfully that he almost sizzled. He hugged his knees to his chest, put his head down and cried openly.

"Why are you crying?" asked Wren. "You should be happy."

"I don't belong here," Cyan bawled. He cupped his face with his hands.

"That's exactly what you needed." Wren clapped his hands once. "Empathy! Contrition! For too long you've thought only of yourself and not cared about how your actions affected others. That's been your fatal flaw, Cyan."

"I'm sorry," Cyan murmured into his palms. It was an apology not directed at anyone in particular. Rather, it was meant for the universe.

"I know you are," Wren said, putting a hand on Cyan's shoulder. "If you weren't, you wouldn't be here now." He tucked a hand under Cyan's arm and helped him stand. "Come with me."

Wren held out an arm to show Cyan the way. The doors at the top of the gleaming double staircase cracked open and a burst of golden light poured into the room. Cyan's heart leapt in his chest. The light felt warm, comforting, inviting—it was all just too right.

Arm in arm as the best of friends, Wren and Cyan ascended the stairs.

* * *

An army of bruised and battle-wounded men huddled in a tent around Cyan's body after the fighting had ended. The field doctors opined he was dead long before his men found him. The arrow halfway buried into his chest had ripped his heart in two, killing him instantly.

Something about Cyan's body puzzled them, and even the doctors could not make sense of it. When they found his body Cyan's lips were pulled back in a placid, satisfied grin, as if he knew something they didn't.

Years later, after the war was long over, that smile was expertly captured on the face of the equestrian statue erected in Cyan's hometown.

THE END

DISCOVER OTHER BOOKS AVAILABLE THROUGH DARKWATER SYNDICATE

I Was A Teenage Cuban Arsonist!
By: R. Perez de Pereda

Ramiro and his two older brothers get into trouble, discover girls, and inadvertently burn down the family farm. Upon arriving in Miami, he is recruited into a counterrevolutionary movement formed to oppose Castro. In a blink, Ramiro goes from penniless immigrant to soldier of fortune. *I Was A Teenage Cuban Arsonist* is a powerful memoir of Ramiro Perez's adventures growing up in pre-revolutionary Cuba, and later, as an exile in Miami.

Chasing Blood
By: R. Perez de Pereda

A briefcase full of money lies on the floor.

Would you take it?

Ryan Cantril learned early on to fight for his keep, and sometimes just to keep what he earned. Now in his thirties, the self-proclaimed king of the sucker punch fights to keep the cash he rightfully stole from a powerful crime syndicate—and if he's lucky, his life.

The Gullwing Odyssey
By: Antonio Simon, Jr.

A four-time award winning fantasy/comedy adventure. When an unusual assignment sends Marco overseas, he finds himself dodging pirates and a hummingbird with an appetite for human brains. Little does he know the fate of a civilization may rest upon his shoulders. In spite of himself, Marco becomes the hero he strives not to be.

Your Life Sucks, Buy This Book:
Transform Your Life In Ways You Never Thought Possible Or Ethical
By: Cavanaugh Kellough Sweeny

Now a national bestseller (of no place on Earth), this book contains Cavanaugh K. Sweeny's proven Your Life Sucks, Buy This Book system of life fulfillment. Whether it's your career, your spiritual development, or your degree of personal fulfillment, the information in this book will do absolutely nothing towards making your life better, but your money will get Mr. Sweeny that much closer to buying another vacation home. A must-read for fans of self-help and business development books, or CEO's who love a good laugh.

ABOUT THE AUTHOR

Born in Cuba in 1941, Ramiro Perez de Pereda has seen it all. Growing up in a time when then-democratic Cuba was experiencing unprecedented foreign investment, he was exposed to the U.S. pop culture items of the day. Among them: pulp fiction magazines, which young Ramiro avidly read and collected. Far and away, his favorites were the *Conan the Barbarian* stories by Robert E. Howard.

Ramiro, now retired from the corporate life, is a grandfather of five. He devotes himself to his family, his writing, and the occasional pen-and-ink sketch. He writes poetry and short fiction under the name R. Perez de Pereda.

Ramiro serves Darkwater Syndicate as its Head Acquisitions Editor—he heads the department, he does not collect heads, which is a point he has grown quite fond of making. Indeed, it's one reason he likes his job so much.

This is his first novel.

ABOUT
DARKWATER SYNDICATE

We are Darkwater Syndicate—the publishing company with a defense contractor's name—and we kick ass. Founded in 2008, we are a full-service indie publisher of fantasy, science fiction, horror, comedy, and thrillers. From our headquarters in Miami Lakes, Florida, we promote indie authors and offer the best in reading entertainment.

Join us on Patreon.

Visit us at www.DarkwaterSyndicate.com.

Follow us on Facebook and Twitter.